PRAISE FOR *TRAVELERS*

PRAISE FOR *STARFALL*,
A NEL BENTLY UNIVERSE SHORT STORY

D0813831

OTHER BOOKS BY
V. S. HOLMES

*forthcoming

DRIFTERS

BOOK TWO OF THE NEL BENTLY BOOKS

V.S. HOLMES

 AMPHIBIAN PRESS

This is a work of fiction. All of the characters, organizations, and events portrayed in this novel are either products of the author's imagination or are used fictitiously.

DRIFTERS

Amphibian Press
P.O. Box 163
West Peterborough NH
03468

www.amphibianpressbooks.com
www.vs-holmes.com
ISBN : 978-0-9983332-0-5

For Paleoman, who runs as fast as I do

DRIFTERS

V.S. HOLMES

1

"Lucy, I'm home." Nel's whisper echoed through the deserted house. She dropped her bag on the bench by the door and sighed. Her body ached from the hours of air travel. She loved flying, but eighteen hours was too long for her to really enjoy the experience.

She deposited her Trader Joe's bag on the counter and extracted a sweating beer before meandering through the house. Lights did little to warm the empty house as she made sure everything was how she had left it a week ago. She turned on her desk lamp and ran her fingers over the stack of half finished lesson plans. She had another week before she really had to work on them. The thought of going back was unbearable. She turned the light off again and stepped out onto the back stoop. She had a poor excuse for a patio, mostly brown grass and plastic lawn furniture, but it was hers. Her knees cracked as she sank onto the steps. The peepers sang their last love songs of the season. Sunlight dripped across the sky above the scraggly pines between her joke of a lawn and the wetlands beyond. It was cool, compared to Chile, but still warm enough to sit in just shorts and a tee. She tipped back her beer, enjoying the microbrew she missed all summer. She smiled when she felt Mikey's echo ease down beside her. "Last gasp of summer, eh? One week left of freedom before we're expected to be adults again."

She almost heard his snarky response. *"If you had your way you'd still be a party-hard grad student with a different girl in your bed each night."*

"If I had my way you wouldn't be dead." She glanced over. The spot beside her was empty, the porch clammy from the morning's rain. She tugged her phone from her pocket and switched off airplane mode. Two texts from Martos, and a phone call from the college. She thumbed through to where Lin's number was, in case she had missed it before. Nothing. She dialed before she could think better of it.

"We're sorry, the number you are trying to reach is no longer in service. Please check the number and try again."

She pursed her lips and tossed the phone across the porch. Lin and Chile and spacecraft were worlds away from her now, a distant dream that, despite bordering on being a nightmare for half the time, she didn't want to wake from. The darkening sky was dotted with clouds. *See that blue star, somewhere between here and there.* Her groceries thawed on the counter, but she couldn't bring herself to get up to make dinner. "It's not fair, you know." She addressed the expanse of dry grass, as if Mikey still stood there, poking at the fire they always lit at the end of summer vacation. "First you, then Lin? I'm the one that's supposed to do the leaving."

♠

Nel hastily shoved her lesson plans into her messenger bag as Martos pulled in the drive. She should have had far more done by now. Just looking at Mikey's handwriting made her want to scream. The kettle started to mutter to itself and she set about making tea.

Martos wheeled into the kitchen. "I can't believe they finally paved that road. First time in years I didn't fear for my alignment."

Nel laughed and jerked a nod at the kitchen counter. "I've got some salad stuff set out already, if you're interested. And kettle's just boiled."

"I'll pass on the salad—dentist appointment later. Roobios would be lovely, though."

She grinned to herself as she filled his already prepared mug. He never changed. She leaned on the counter across from him after making her coffee. "So what did you want to talk about?"

"I wanted to see how you're doing. School's just around the corner and you haven't been to the office once."

She looked down. "I'm doing all right. It's kind of hard to be there."

"I know." He dipped his head to catch her eye. "But you might want to get that over with before we're swarmed by students."

"Martos, the anthropology department will never be in danger of being swarmed." She offered him a smile she did not feel. "What are you going to do about North American Lithic Analysis and Anthropology of Food? Two of our students need those to graduate on time."

"I found an adjunct to take over your intro courses. You'll take over Mikey's stuff."

Nel winced. As if reading his notes wasn't hard enough. "And his grad students?"

"Are now mine."

"Right." She stared at her coffee, wondering absently if the milk was sour and that's why her stomach churned.

"You have three weeks before classes actually start, but I need to know if you can handle this."

"I handle everything you throw at me, Martos."

"I'm not worried about whether you'll get it done. I know you will. I'm worried if you'll break in the process. I've barely spoken to you since you came back, I don't really know what happened down there. And then yesterday morning I get this on my desk." He handed her a slim envelope.

Nel drew out the papers, eyeing him warily. The forms indicated her interest in publishing her findings from Los Cerros Esperando VII and requested involved parties to begin compiling their data for publication. Though the signature was hers, she was certain she had never written this up. *Thanks for throwing me under the bus, Lin.* "What about it?"

"Well you've barely begun excavation on the site, and as far as I know you had your permits revoked twice, the second time permanently. Why do you want to publish this mess?"

Because I was exhausted and promised someone I would. "What happened down there is really complicated. I can't even explain it; wonder if I'm dreaming half the time."

"Death is a complex thing, Nel, and I don't think you've ever dealt with this kind of death."

"Peers have died before."

"Mikey wasn't just your peer and we both know it. Stop the tough-girl act. You didn't even make it to Phase III. If you think this will somehow give Mikey a good name, I'll remind you that his name is fine. Better than yours in a lot of cases."

She squirmed under his warm, steady eyes. She hated when someone saw through her. "I know. But there's more to it, Martos. It's politically complicated. Mikey was just the beginning." She chewed on her lip, debating how much he could hear without threatening to commit her.

"Two days ago I got a phone call from your backers. It wasn't the woman I normally speak with. They said she was on a new project."

"What else?" Nel forced her tone to be neutral.

"Politically complicated is fine, Nel, but this is me you're talking to. Are these people dangerous?"

"Dangerous? Like a mob?" Nel scoffed. When Martos's expression did not change, she looked down. It was possible. She had seen their weapons, knew first hand their influence. She was certain it was just a fraction of their actual might. "Honestly, I don't know. They have deep pockets and long arms. I also think they will do far more good than harm."

"What about tenure? Are you still interested in that? You were going to apply for it this fall, but the deadline is almost passed."

"Of course I still want it! And sorry I'm a bit late. I've had a funeral to deal with. I was planning on tenure, on running another site with Mikey. I was going to start my own field school out of the university." She looked away. "I was going to do a lot of things."

"You make it sound like you were the one that died down there. You life's not over." He drew out another stack of papers, this one the much more familiar application for tenure.

"Not over, just different, and I've got to come to grips with that."

Martos nodded once in his crisp, yet caring way. "Here. You have a week to look over things. Apply for tenure when you're ready, but don't forget your dreams just because you're grieving."

She scanned the papers, though she didn't really retain most of the information. "Thanks, Martos." She flashed him a tired smile.

"Nel, do you have anyone to talk to? Are you seeing anyone, professionally or romantically in whom you can confide?"

"Not really. I was, I mean, but things are still really new and she's got her own stuff. I met her down in Chile."

"Long distance isn't your style. More like arm's length."

She glared at him, but he was dead right. "Ouch. And it's not long distance. She came down to smooth things out after they attacked him." She couldn't bring herself to say the names, not yet. "Her name is Lin."

"Ms. Nalawangsa? I've spoken with her on the phone. Sounded young and passionate." His delicate brow rose. "I suppose that is your style." He straightened and folded his jacket over his arm. "I've got go. Appointments in twenty, care to walk me out?"

She hummed in response and popped his empty mug into the sink before following him out the door. "Thanks for stopping by. I'll be in tomorrow to talk to the board about the site and the semester. You'll be there?"

"I will." He hoisted himself into his Hyundai and collapsed his chair. "You talked to any of the students yet?"

"I've emailed back and forth with a few of them. Why?"

"Well, sometimes helping someone else grieve can help you. Hearing their stories and thoughts might bring you some peace, knowing you weren't the only one who loved him." He pointed to the house. "Look over those papers. You've worked hard and could do this." He shut the door with a smile and pulled out of the drive.

Nel waved him off before returning to the kitchen to stare at the paperwork. *Is this the life I want?* Martos's words about talking to someone irked her. She wanted to claim the of course she had friends, had family to talk to, but it had just been her and Mikey for so long. Sometimes she forgot where he ended and she began.

2

Rain meandered down Nel's front windows—the picture of her mood. She checked the clock again. 6:43. There was no way she could go back to sleep, but her meeting wasn't for another four hours. The coffee in her mug was tepid and oily. She moved into the living room and paused at the two boxes on the mantelpiece. "Hey, Mikey." The lines on her face softened. "Hey, Dad." She thought about calling her mom, but Mindi would be getting ready to go to work, and calling her outside of their usual schedule would only worry her.

"Nel, get a grip on yourself. You're too angry to pull off the brooding mystery shtick."

She downed her coffee. "You're right." It took a minute to change into the clothes she had picked out for her meeting. Work boots weren't professional, but the faded black women's Timberlands looked fine under jeans. She slung a few things into her bag next to the ignored tenure papers and shoved out the door. She tripped over the package on her stoop. *Probably the revoking of my funding.* She slid the padded envelope into her bag without looking at it, and jumped into her blue Nissan Frontier. The engine rattled to life and she patted the steering wheel. "I missed you too, Samus."

Nel didn't enjoy how most people drove in the rain, but it would wash the summer's dust from her truck, and that brought a smile to her face. She lived twenty minutes outside of town if she took the highway, which she never did. As much as she loved driving, back roads were infinitely better. In her first year living in Jasper Hill she got hopelessly lost every time she pulled out of her driveway. After months of refusing to get on Route 190, though, her stubbornness paid off. She could find her way home from almost anywhere, and see nice scenery while she was at it. Her cell rattled in the cup holder in the center console, and she sighed. Probably Martos, making sure she wasn't going to bail on her meeting. She slid her thumb across the screen. "Yeah?"

"Hey, honey, how're you doing?"

"Oh, hey, Mom. All right."

"How was your flight? When'd you get in?"

Nel grinned at the barrage of questions. Her mom was nothing if not curious. As much as they all joked that Nel was the clone of her father, the older she got, the more she realized that she was really a mixture of her parents. "I'm driving, so I can't really talk, but I got in Saturday night. Flight was fine. Had some turbulence and stuff, and a crying baby, but that was it." She could almost picture her flight-terrified mother's shudder.

"Glad I wasn't there. Where are you headed?"

"To the school. I have a meeting with the department. Martos wants me to bring up tenure, and I'm sure I'll hear a ton about the site and safety and responsibility."

"They don't actually think it was your fault, do they?" Rustling clothes and the sound of clinking dishes told Nel her mom was unloading the dishwasher.

"I don't know what they think, really, but I'm sure it's not pretty. The problem is the situation was dangerous, and I had kids down there. I'm kinda stressed about it all."

Her mom hummed in sympathy and the background noise stopped as she paused to focus on the conversation. "You call me afterward, all right? We can talk it out. And maybe you can come down for dinner this week?"

Nel smiled. Her mom was a good listener. "Yeah, I'll call. Not sure about dinner, things are really gearing up for the semester, and I'm supposed to take on a bunch of Mikey's stuff."

"I can kick Bill out of the house; send him to play billiards with the fire department guys."

"How does Thursday sound?" Nel offered. She loved seeing her mom, and a meal she didn't have to cook herself was a rarity. It wasn't always worth dealing with her stepdad and his opinions.

Nel's mom snorted. "I thought so. Thursday's good for me. I'll let you know later if I can shoo him out that night. When is your meeting out?"

"Noon. I'll call you then?"

"All right, sweetie. Good luck. Love you!"

"Love you, too." Nel tapped her phone and dropped it back into the cup holder. Her stomach wasn't as tight as before. The only person who settled her mind as much as Mikey was her mom. She spun the wheel and turned down University Ave. The broad street was separated by a row of flowering trees and abstract art installations. An undulating fountain stood under the broad arched entrance to the college. It was sputtering and green, as it usually was in the summer, but in two weeks she was sure it would sparkle. Nel slammed the brakes on as a group of boys stumbled into the road on their way across campus. "Get out of the fucking road, you idiots!"

One flipped her off, then saw her professor-parking pass and scooted after his friends.

"Yeah, that's right you little asshole." She turned into the parking lot and found a spot in the shade. She pressed her forehead against the rim of the steering wheel and drew a breath. She shouldn't have anything to worry about.

"What's the worst case scenario?" Mikey always had a way to rationalize her out of a panic.

"They fire me."

"So what? You've got the creds. You can teach plenty of places. Maybe not as hip as UNNE, but still something."

She steadied her thoughts before tugging her bag from the passenger seat and heading towards the sprawling multi-addition Social Studies building. She had fifteen minutes to collect herself and drop her things at her desk. Every thought grew heavy and frantic as Nel shoved the doors open. Six months ago, the only goal on her career list that had yet to be checked off was attaining a tenured position. Working with a smaller university like UNNE that focused more on published papers and teaching ability than seniority brought her goal that much closer. It hurt that she might not achieve it now, depending on the meeting. It hurt worse, though, that a large part of her no longer cared. It was the same part that howled into the void in her chest where Mikey used to be. She strode through the History wing and into the breezeway between the original part of the building and the first addition. She pulled the package from her stoop out with a sigh. *Right, because I want to read the details of all my permits being revoked.* Still, it would distract her from the looming shadow of her meeting. The package was heavy, and decorated with multiple stamps and seals. None were of her local post office.

DR. ANNALISE BENTLY
c/o LIN NALAWANGSA
IDH CANADIAN HEADQUARTERS,
4 ENDEAVOUR LN

OROMOCTO, NB, E2V 4T9

Nel frowned. *She can drop a package at my stoop, but can't respond to a text? And why send this to my house rather than my office?* She tugged the tab, expecting a thick document. Instead, a cheap cell phone dropped into her hand. It was new, and off-brand, the kind that box-stores sold minute cards for. She frowned, but flipped it open and held down the power button. The chime was tinny. It was fully charged and had prepaid minutes through the end of the month. A cartoon UFO decorated the background. *What the fuck?*

She thumbed to the message box. There was only one, from a contact titled, "Mothership." She rolled her eyes and looked at the message:

TEXT 'RECEIVED' AND YOUR SURNAME WHEN THIS ARRIVES.

She did as it asked and trotted up the stairs to the lobby of the Anthropology wing, barely looking away from the phone.

"Dr. Annalise Bently?"

Nel glanced up. Two campus security officers blocked the doorway to her department. A state trooper stood a step in front, holding up his ID. "Dr. Bently is fine."

"Ma'am, I'm Officer Thomson. You oversaw the Los Cerros Esperando VII this past summer, correct?"

"Yes, I did." Her nerves screamed at her.

"The Chilean police found a body yesterday." He glanced at the students milling around. "You need to come with us."

"I haven't been on site for over a month." The new phone buzzed in her hand. Her fingers tightened around it.

"The body has your DNA on it, ma'am. We need to bring you in."

"For arrest?"

"Come quietly and you won't make a scene in front of your students."

Adrenaline exploded through her body. *I'm wanted for murder. Lin said there were no bodies. She said I'd be safe.* Her eyes flicked up to the cop. She slid the envelope into her bag before glancing at the phone. An incoming text opened on the screen.

RUN

And she did.

3

Nel didn't know what she was doing, only that she wasn't a killer, and the only person who seemed to know what was going on had told her to run.

Like all university buildings, this one had a multitude of exits in case of emergency. Nel dashed back down the hall and into a back stair well. Her feet barely touched the stairs as she half-slid down them, her weight supported by her hands on the banister. The door at the bottom banged open, then shut as she burst onto the quad. The campus was almost deserted. "Fuck." *It'd be easier if there were a butt load of students to hide in.* She crossed campus at a run, hammering on her key fob as she went. She jumped into her truck, peeling out of the parking lot while shutting her door. She pulled out in front of a Prius and swung across two lanes to head towards the highway.

She mentally ran through the things in the back of her truck. She didn't have time to stop at home, and it would only be a matter of minutes before they caught up to her. *Picking a bright blue truck wasn't a good idea, in hindsight.* She downshifted and roared up the entrance ramp onto 112 North. Her field pack was tucked in the tool box in the bed. Other than that, she was shit out of luck. The phone tucked between her thighs pinged insistently. She fumbled it open, ignoring the voice telling her not to text and drive.

MOVE NORTH TOWARD CANADIAN HEADQUARTERS

"To Oromoncto? Are you fucking kidding me? You want me to cross a border while on the run. You people are idiots." She snapped the phone closed and threw it in her cup holder before pulling out her own cell. The suggestion was ridiculous, but her mind already whirled. The border wasn't all fences and checkpoints, but she certainly couldn't drive there, or even hitchhike. Her shaking hand thumbed to her mother's speed dial and pressed the speaker phone.

"Hey, you've reached Mindi. I'm off doing something awesome, but I'll get back to you as soon as I can."

Nel swallowed hard. "Hey, mom. Something's come up. I didn't make it to my meeting, and I won't be able to call you later. Or for a while, really. I love you, please don't worry. I'm sorry. I love you." She hung up and flicked on airplane mode, then turned the phone off for good measure. She wasn't sure if they could track her through the GPS, but she wasn't going to risk it.

She ducked into the faster lane, leveling off at a steady 75 MPH while she watched the exits crawl by. Another minute brought her across the border into Vermont. She took the first exit and turned right, onto a winding back road that had once led to Mikey's house. She knew it well enough to trust going 40 MPH. State troopers might not. *Besides, Samus can take the ruts.* She popped into four wheel drive and rattled ahead. The road wound up hill to a T intersection. She slowed to a stop and glanced between her two options. *This is so stupid. I should have just let them take me in. It's not like I'm guilty.*

Her mind turned to her last night with Lin. The shed had been chaos. But she remembered the feeling of the sharpened edge of her trowel sinking into flesh. *I can't be guilty.*

Route 9 led down towards Brattleboro, or up towards Wilmington. She spun the wheel, pointing the car east. The still-summer air buffeted her thorough the open window, bringing the squeal of distant police sirens. She was far from America's Most Wanted, but she wouldn't risk anything. She couldn't. Overhead, power lines looped like ugly party streamers. Her eyes traced the line of structures marching up the swath cut through the trees. *No one's on power line corridors. At least not often.* She had hiked her fare share doing CRM after undergrad. She couldn't leave her car where they'd follow, though.

The sirens grew closer.

Her wheels spun, dirt rising as she peeled to a stop just past a bridge. The river meandered towards the Connecticut, passing under the power lines before curling back towards the border. "Fuck it." She pulled onto the shoulder, tucking her truck into a pull off by a run-down park bench. She thrust the package into her field pack and scooped the mess of forgotten things from her center consol into one of the pockets. Her new cell phone slid into a grimy plastic baggie from an old lunch. Then she tossed the keys under the seat and manually locked the doors.

She sprinted toward the river as the first cruiser peeled onto the road after her. She slung her pack across her chest and scrambled into the shallows. Her first instinct was to hide under the bridge, but she already lost her head start. If they saw her truck and she was anywhere nearby the game would be up. She slipped under the bridge, trying to count the sirens. One, but there might be more. She knew she was far from dangerous, but they didn't. She edged into the deep channel in the center of the river until her feet were swept from under her.

Her chest heaved and she forced herself to take several deep breaths. With a last gasp she forced the air from her lungs and sank. The current swept her away. The silty water burned her eyes, but she watched as the shadow of the bridge was replaced with glaring light. She was grateful that the current, though strong, wasn't violent. She stayed under until her lungs burned, until her body could take no more, then stayed under another fifteen seconds.

Air billowed into her chest as Nel burst to the surface. The water flung her against a submerged tree and she shoved towards the bank. Broken wood gouged her arm, but she hung on, tucked into the camouflage of the tangled tree limbs. The cruiser had indeed stopped. She could hear the faint crackle of pagers, followed by the shattering of glass. She groaned. *Not my fucking truck.* She had hoped locking it would slow them down, even for a minute. *Clearly I was wrong.* She dragged herself along the tree to the bank.

The pull off was hidden by the guard rails. She moved slowly, wincing each time water sluiced from her jeans. The corridor was another hundred meters downstream. She tucked herself into the woods, avoiding any dead branches she could. Her waterlogged clothes dragged at her legs, tripping her far more than she liked. Finally, she emerged onto the corridor and crossed to the opposite tree line. She needed to keep moving, but if anyone saw her now it wouldn't be a stretch to figure out she was a fugitive.

She stumbled. Was that what she was now? She could have told herself she had run without thinking, that she had panicked. There was enough adrenaline in her body for her to almost believe the latter. *But I did think.* Her understanding of the world ended with Mikey. But now there was this other person, this impossible woman who seemed too young and too old at once. Nel's mind may have been spinning but so was she and with the chaos around her, Lin was the only thing Nel could see clearly. *So when her people tell me to run, I just do it?*

Daylight was precious, but so was a plan. The racket of searching echoed between the trees as the cops scoured the woods and road. Moving in wet jeans was almost impossible. She knew they would call for backup when they failed to find her in the woods surrounding her car. *I have a few minutes to regroup.* She removed her sodden boots and stripped down to boxers and her tank top. She balled the wet clothes into one of the waterproof pockets in her pack. She hated to wear wet socks and boots, but her feet weren't tough enough for the roadfill and broken glass of the access road.

"What do you think, Mikey? Deer blind or party spot?" It was a favorite game from when they did walkovers, each betting which of the more modern evidence of human inhabitants they would find first. She usually went for the party spots.

"Deer blind sure would do you more good now."

She shrugged on her pack and found the access road. The corridor didn't abut any homes for another few miles, and the loose gravel would hide her footprints better than any soft forest loam. It took another forty minutes for her heart to stop pounding. Though curiosity gnawed in her stomach, she refused to look at the phone. Deciphering the Institute's convoluted message would be her task later, when she was able to rest. She didn't think about how many miles she had left to hike, only that she had another step to take, and then another.

By 2:00 her stomach's rumbling was loud enough that Nel was sure the cops could hear it. *I need to figure out something for food, and soon. I can go a few days, but not without a plan.* The corridors were lousy with wild raspberries and blackberries, but they would require a healthy dip in the stream before Nel would eat them. *Last thing I need is to eat the nasty defoliant all over this place.* She passed a teenagers' fire pit, complete with a destroyed couch and smashed beer bottles, but after a few cursory kicks to the dirt, it yielded nothing of use. Despite having worked all summer, her legs ached. *I do not have the body of twenty-year-old Nel anymore.*

She knew the roads almost by heart, but walking the corridor was like seeing everything from the other side, and it threw off her sense of direction. Not to mention traveling by foot was far slower than she expected. She was still damp, and she needed to find somewhere to gather herself. The sound of sirens was long gone. The last sign of civilization, besides the fire pit, had been a house just before noon. The corridor swept upwards along a high ridge bordering a reservoir to the west. A huge pile of boulders spilled down the slope, both glacial erratics and the results of a more recent push-pile. *Rock shelters worked for paleo-people. They'll work for me, too.*

One larger rock sat at the base of the pile. Years of ice had broken it asunder, and half had begun a slow slide down the hill. This left two walls perfect for building a temporary shelter. Smudges of smoke marred the stone from use in the past few years, and several beer bottles decorated the mossy granite. Nel plopped down at the fire pit. The ash was faint and the soot covering the rocks more grey than black. *Good, they won't be back tonight, at any rate.* It took a moment to clear the leaves and sticks from around the pit and pile them in the center of the bowl of rocks. As much as lighting a fire was a dangerous option, hiking mostly naked or wet was worse, even at the end of summer. A sapling served as a rack to hang her pants and shirt. A tangled mess of a dead tree had snagged on the rocks, and Nel erected the driest pieces in a pyramid around the tinder. Another sweep of the surrounding ground made sure she wouldn't start a brush fire. The sodden front pocket of her pack produced a lighter. A minute's clicking finally dried the flint and tinder of the igniter enough to light her campfire. She watched the flames test the wood with their orange tongues. Her body was jelly, but she couldn't rest now, even with a small shelter set up.

She settled into the crevice of the rock and upended her pack at her feet. Her field kit was sparse, but at least held sharp tools, a compass, and water bottle. The center console provided a handful of hot sauce packets, someone's melted eyeliner, several wads of chewed gum, and a few crumpled dollar bills. She would need food, and a map would be helpful, but she couldn't risk going to a store so soon after running. The small pocket of her pack held a few expired peanut butter and honey packets. Between that and the hot sauce, she would have to make it a week at least.

She groaned. Still, her clothes would be dry by morning, and she had managed a fire. It wouldn't do to have one every night, but for now, she was hell-bent on enjoying what she could. She had just nodded off against the rough, warming stone, when her phone buzzed.

BENTLY. CONFIRM LOCATION.

She rolled her eyes and typed a response, grateful that they couldn't hear her snarky tone.

SAFE AND IN HIDING. NOT MANY SUPPLIES

The response was immediate:

YOU NEED TO MAKE YOUR WAY NORTH, WE NEED YOU TO BE AT FORT APAJIAQ IN OROMOCTO.

She sighed at the reiteration. "I told you, you fuckers are nuts. How am I going to go almost 600 miles on foot with half a dozen condiment packets and one pair of underwear?" Instead she responded that she would try. Either that was enough, or they were tired of dealing with her. Her phone stayed silent for the rest of the evening.

She curled up in the crevice, pulling some dry leaves and a branch over her body. It was going to be cold, but the fire helped. Her body was exhausted, but her mind raced laps around her skull. *Why do they think I did it? What other evidence do they have? How'd my DNA end up on the body?*

Did I actually do it?

4

Morning could not come soon enough. Her back was one solid cramp and she balled herself into as small a shape as possible to stay warm. *That's the last time I sleep naked out here.* Still, the night passed without a dozen cops exploding from the woods at her, and that was something. She shoved herself out of her leafy bed, nose wrinkling at the number of bug bites she would discover later. Her jeans were damp, but better than before, and her shirts were dry. The fire smoldered sullenly, not hot enough to cast any real warmth aside from comfort. She repacked her still-damp bag, arranging things in order of necessity.

Next, she reread the text. The list of who it could be was very short, in Nel's mind. It was either the Institute or Lin, and she was fairly certain, however they had left things, that Lin's messages would be friendlier. If they wanted her to come to Oromocto, or anywhere, really, they should send someone. She could stay out of the way of the cops for a while, but certainly not forever. She glanced at the battery. It was almost full, but that wouldn't last long, especially with the spotty signal on most corridors. Texting drained the battery less than a phone call. *Besides, if it was safe to call, wouldn't they have done so already?* She decided to turn it on once a day to check her messages. *No more than that*, she commanded herself.

> SAVING BATTERY. WILL TURN PHONE ON AROUND NOON EST EACH DAY. HEADED NORTH. WOULDN'T MIND A RIDE.

She copied the message and sent it to Lin, though she wasn't sure if the number even worked. Then she powered the phone down. Somehow the descending notes as the screen went black made her feel even more alone. Her stomach was a dull, aching pit between her ribs, but she knew it would get worse before it got better. It wouldn't be safe to brave a town, even a small one used to hikers, for at least a week. Even then, she would need a disguise. Pushing that problem away for future-Nel to handle, she snagged some of the peanut butter from her front pouch. She rolled it in her mouth far longer than necessary, satisfying her mind, if not her stomach. Mist collected in the valley to the left and dotted the gullies in the rolling hills like suspicion rising in her mind. Her steps were steady and slow, a morning's stroll that would have to make her energy last all day. Adrenaline had worn off sometime during the night, finally allowing her to sleep. Now, though, she suffered the consequences of bruises and torn muscles obtained while under the raging influence of panic.

She hiked up to the closest power line pole. Metal plates imbedded in the blackened wood designated it Structure 231. Another noted that it belonged to Northern Lights Energy Company. She wrote it down in the battered notebook from the bottom of her pack and shouldered her things again. It was going to be a long day, the first of many that she was sure would erode her spirit as fast as they ate at her bones.

"Well, Mikey, I've finally got a reason to be angry."

"You always did, Dirt-butt. I just wanted you to figure out why."

"I don't really care why now, I just know it's the only thing burning hot enough to keep me from getting killed."

She could almost feel the warmth as he smiled, feel the air move as he fell into step beside her. *"That's it, Nel. Stay alive. Keep walking, keep fighting, and stay alive."*

♦

Nel's boots thudded onto the compacted dirt of someone's lawn just before noon. It was still overcast, but most of the mist had burned off. The house was tucked up on a hill, a hundred meters away from the corridor, probably near the roadside. Nel's steps faltered. She was tired and hungry, and should have known better than to stumble onto someone's property.

It was a Thursday, so perhaps everyone would be at work or school. The grass was scrubbier on the edge of the lawn, and Nel kept to the border of briars and high grasses. She lengthened her stride to look less exhausted, more like she belonged. As soon as she hit the trees, she cut back onto the overgrown corridor. *That was too close.* The gravel crunched under her shoes and she tugged her phone from her pocket. It must have been close to noon. There was a chance the house was the only one in the area that crossed the corridor, but she highly doubted it. The phone muttered its greeting and she held it against her chest as she climbed higher and the messages rolled in.

Both were from "Mothership," one listing the address of the base, the next asking for her location again. She had asked for a ride, but just giving away her location made her skin crawl. She had no way of knowing if the cops could track her, or if the line was secure. She jogged up to the power line pole ahead. The metal tag designated it Structure 1302. Though lines had come in and out twice since her escape, she still seemed to be using Northern Lights's corridor. After a moment's thought, she opened the message again and tapped a reply:

1302AURORA.

It was cryptic enough to make her feel safe, though she knew she was probably underestimating the intelligence of those tracking her.

Her stomach growled an angry counterpoint to her footsteps on the gravel. At first she countered her hunger by drinking as much water as she could hold, but even that wasn't helping now, and she was dangerously low on electrolytes. Her muscles stood stark without their usual padding. Her water bottle bounced off her pack with a hollow thump. She needed to find a stream, soon. *Maybe some berries, too.* She snorted. "My doctor would be so proud—no beer, red meat, or coffee for days!"

"*I doubt even your hippie-dippie-crunch doctor had a law-enforced hunger strike in mind.*"

Nel rolled her eyes, steps speeding up at the sound of running water. The day already promised to be hot, and no water since the night before was not a good way to start. The rivulet that greeted her over the next rise was a cruel tease. The rocks were slick with orange and green slime, and only the very center moved with any degree of speed. The stagnant puddles where the water eddied glistened with a chemical sheen. She eyed the surrounding plants. Most were brown and dead, and the grasses had a sickly undertone to their brittle green.

Pollution means humans. She followed the burbling water to where it originated. It looked like a spring, sputtering from rocks decorated with brown moss, but judging by the foul smell, Nel guessed it originated somewhere uphill and dipped in and out of the ground. A small cleared area smelled of stale beer and grease. A haphazard fire pit crouched in the middle of the circle of trees. A metal ladder led up one of the larger trunks. *Redneck hunting lodge.* There were a few empty bottles of lighter fluid, which accounted for the acrid smell of the water.

"Well, it might be a shining example of human carelessness, but I'll take it." The heat of the day neared its peak. She held a palm over the coals. They were cold, but the charcoal was new and hadn't been rained on during the storm two days before. *Thank fuck it's not early morning, or I might have found some unwanted company.* Hunting wasn't something Nel had ever tried herself, but she had a vague recollection of the various seasons from dating a woman from upstate in college. *It should be bow-hunting soon, or maybe the old-fashion guns?* She did a quick circuit of the clearing, hoping for some trash that she could repurpose. The ladder disappeared into the still leafed branches of the tree, but she assumed a blind perched there with a view of the corridor. The blind was little more than a rickety metal chair and a plywood platform covered in what looked like spat chewing tobacco juice and pitch.

At this rate, Nel would have been happy to find a warm, flat beer forgotten somewhere in the clearing. She gave up all hope after finding a nasty pile of cloth in a hole that was clearly used for a latrine. "Seriously, Lin, I don't know why you bother. Humans are disgusting and hopeless." A forgotten apple tree from some long-overgrown farm afforded her a shady spot a hundred meters from the blind. She tucked herself into the roots, head pillowed on a clump of grass, and closed her eyes. Though it should have been impossible with a root digging into her left kidney and a rock under her shoulder, she felt her eyes lidding with exhaustion.

The phone buzzed a second later. It wasn't a reply from "Mothership," but a new message from a strange number.

HEY ARE YOU SAFE?
MISS YOU
L

Nel's brows shot up. Of course Lin would text her now, when everything was on the line, when Nel's faith was being tested more than ever. *When I might be a murderer.* The woman seemed to be the world champ of the elastic-band method of dating. *Or whatever fucked up relationship thing we've got going on.* There wasn't a word for a co-worker one slept with before both of them started running from the law. She almost ignored the message, almost deleted it. The number was a new one, different from the one she had tried to call more times than she was frankly comfortable admitting. Instead, she typed a response and powered the phone down before she could think better of it.

SAFE ENOUGH

5

The sun pierced through the turning leaves, finding Nel's eyes with vicious excitement. "Ugh, Mikey, close the shades. I'm up, I promise." The wind muttering through the branches was her only response. The smell of pine sap, damp soil, and her own sweat jolted Nel back into reality. She groaned and sat up. Despite the cramped space between two halves of a split boulder, she had overslept. The sun marched towards its peak, and Nel guessed it was closer to noon than dawn. She stretched, using the beams of the blind to help crack her back, before dumping her bag onto the floor. It had become a ritual the past four days, something to keep her feeling in charge, despite the incredible lack of control. One packet of peanut butter and two of hot sauce.

She rued the day she tossed her other cell phone, though it was decidedly for the best. "I wish I had a map, something to tell me where the hell I am." She assumed she had made it to south of St. Johnsbury. Her starved brain was slow to remind her that she had crossed the Connecticut river into New Hampshire the morning before. She tucked the packets away and finished off her water. Today she would find a town and something approaching solid food.

She shimmed down the blind's ladder, wincing as her impact rocketed up her legs and pounded in her knees. This escapade did nothing to help her body. After a few minutes of walking she reached the edge of a small pond where the corridor passed over a road. It was a broad, paved road, with a long passing lane. A white state sign designated it 302. Moreover, one of the smaller rural roads joined it just to the west and a battered green sign told her where the closest forms of civilization were. "Bethlehem, two miles, Littleton, three. Bethlehem it is." She hoisted her bag higher and grinned into the sun. "Your gospel-loving ass must be getting a kick out of this one, eh?"

"Only if you get kicked out of some hotel and are made to sleep in a shed."

"Yeah, like they'd even let me in the front door to ask, the way I look." She winced. There were plenty of hiking trails up here, but she still worried about explaining away her appearance. She paused under the sign and dug out a bandana and the further-melted eyeliner. The backside of the sign provided enough reflection to darken her blonde eyelashes and brows and tuck most of her hair out of sight. She squinted. She would either look homeless or like a total hippie. *And one of those is kind of true, right now.* Another glance gave her no more confidence than the first, and she set off downhill. School was back in session, and the leaves had yet to pop. Nel was grateful for the quieter roads. The outskirts were much like other small northern towns— fields turned camp grounds and gas stations. Further in, the houses were expansive and old, but reeked of former money. What qualified as the main drag perched on the crest of a hill. A newer building called Indian Brook Trading Company boasted a collection of strange found-metal sculptures and further uphill was a tiny gas station. *Game face, Bently.* She patted her bandana, pulled on a smile and ducked inside.

The woman at the counter looked as worn as Nel felt, albeit cleaner. She shot Nel a vacant greeting without looking up from her sudoku book. Though tiny, the store was packed with the usual combination of snacks, car accessories and fluids, a tiny first-aid shelf, and glass cases filled with hot dogs and pizza. A yellow sign spinning lazily under the AC vent told Nel that pizza was $1.99 and two hog dogs were $2.05.

She double-checked her wadded bills before descending on the hot dogs. She wasn't a fan of them in the strictest sense, but they were suitable vehicles for her favorite condiments. The umami-salt scent of mechanically separated meat hung low over the greasy rollers, punctuated by the sharp, sweet smell of onions and relish. She wasn't even embarrassed when her stomach rumbled over the faint pop radio station. Though the starvation seemed inclined toward the cheddar-wurst, Nel knew that after so many days of hunger, that choice was a one-way ticket to Barf Town, or worse. She piled the safer beef option with two kinds of onions, banana peppers, both varieties of relish, mustard, and ketchup. She carried her precious burden to the counter and peeled two bills free.

"Could you tell me where the nearest Walmart or CVS is?" She wrinkled her nose.

"The campground we're staying at doesn't have shampoo."

The woman gave her a once over, her expression saying that Nel needed a lot more than shampoo. "Littleton. Just a few minutes' drive up 302." She jerked her thumb in a northwesterly direction, back the way Nel had come.

"Right, thanks." She scooped the two hot dogs into her hands and nudged the door open with her foot. *The sign said Littleton was about three miles further north from that intersection. That's about five from here.* Her boots thudded against the hot pavement as she turned left.

She forced herself to take one small bite every two minutes until half of the first hot dog churned in her over-stimulated stomach. She tucked it and the other, whole, one into the plastic bag for later. It wouldn't do any good if she ate too fast and puked everything back up.

Walking along 302 towards the next town was more stressful than the past two days combined. Her heart exploded into panic each time she was buffeted by a car flying past, and she wondered if this would be the driver who recognized her. When she trotted into Littleton proper an hour and a half later, she was ready to never see another car again.

Littleton was a true small New England town—brew-pub, diner, and narrow roads squeezed between renovated brick mill buildings. Looming over the trees and other tourist traps was a sun bleached Walmart sign. *One stop shopping paradise for any fugitive on a budget.* She wove through the parking lot and stepped into too-high air conditioning. Saturday morning was clearly rush hour for cheap shopping. *Hair dye first. Then more food.* She moved along the pharmacy section, tossing ibuprofen and a tooth brush into her basket before stopping by the hair color aisle. She groaned. The cost of hair dye alone would wipe out most of the cash she had, and she hoped to get non-perishable food.

She fumbled the cheapest box open to read the instructions. *Bleach kit?* Nel sighed. She didn't even know what that was. She wished she had been able to grab the various half-used dyes her ex, Tabby, had left in her bathroom cabinet years ago.

"Bad dye job?"

She glanced up at the woman a few feet down. She nodded at Nel's bandana knowingly. "I always try to do it myself, too. Rarely works out." She tugged her ash-blond braid. "Should have seen the oranges I had to go through before I got this."

"I'm looking to go red-brown," Nel finally ground out. "I either end up with orange or purple."

"Try this." The girl swiped a box labeled Warm Chestnut off the shelf. "It's got everything you need in it." She offered a friendly smile.

Nel made a show of reading the back, though she didn't understand half the instructions. "Thanks. You're a big help." She tossed it in her basket. As much as she just wanted to get everything and leave, buying first aid, hair dye, and canned food was probably one of those things that got you flagged for suspicious activity. *Like when Mikey bought condoms, cleaning supplies, and trash bags together and the Speed-Mart guy called the cops.* She grinned and headed for the check out aisle.

An Irving Gas squatted on the corner between 302 and the entrance ramp to 93. It was larger than the mom-and-pop place in Bethlehem, and was busy enough for her to feel unnoticed. *Besides, buying travel supplies from a gas station is less conspicuous.* The bathroom was thankfully a single stall, and Nel double-checked the lock before stripping off her shirt and kerchief. She dumped the pre-mixed dye over her head, working it in haphazardly. Someone knocked.

"It'll be a minute!" Nel rolled her eyes before turning back to the instructions. "'Let it set for twenty minutes'?" she snarled. "I can't stay in here for twenty minutes!" She remembered Tabby sitting in the living room, plastic wrap cocooning her head while waiting for the latest bright color to develop. *Plastic wrap.* She tried the metal cabinet in the corner. It was locked. A box on top offered only extra paper products. Her eyes fell to the waxed paper of the toilet-seat cover. The woman knocked again.

"One minute!" *This is just humiliating.* She worked her hair into a pile atop her head and wrapped the seat covers as tightly as they would go before easing her bandana back over it. At least she would leave looking the same way she entered. She flushed the toilet and shoved the box and dye bottle into her bag before stepping out. She flashed the irritated woman outside a brief smile. "Sorry, that time of the month."

The "No Loitering" sign ushered her to the sunny grass bordering the greasy patch of wetland beyond the parking lot. She fished out the now-squished half of her hot dog and began the careful process of eating.

By the time she was done, her patience for the dye was spent, though she figured it was closer to fifteen minutes than twenty.

The young man at the counter frowned when she stepped up to ask for the bathroom key again. "Hitchhiking?"

"No, sorry, waiting for my ride." She ducked into the bathroom before he could ask her anything else. *So much for not raising suspicions. Should have known gas stations keep a closer eye on things than Wally-world.* She dunked her head in the sink, not bothering to wait until the water was warm. Dye splattered all over the sink, ammonia burning the skin around her eyes. She turned the water off as soon as it ran clear.

She peered into the mirror curiously. *Fuck.* Instead of Warm Chestnut her hair was a brassy auburn. It was not flattering. The ends hadn't spent enough time developing, it seemed, and remained a sullen gold. She pulled her root clippers out with resignation. Thirty seconds later the bottom three inches of her hair floated in the toilet bowl. She tucked her damp, orange pixie cut under the bandana and rinsed what she could of the sink. She didn't bother returning the key, leaving it in the lock. Her eyes caught the sign on the back of the door: *Really, really clean washrooms.*

"Sorry, Irving. Not this time."

It wasn't until she rounded a bend past an old church and a hideously modern elementary school that she noticed the car. It was a hulking black thing, an SUV that looked more like a tank than a mommy-van. It had been parked in the Irving lot, she was pretty sure. Most of the vehicles in the area were battered trucks and souped-up foreign sedans. This was neither, and the plain, government plates were quite enough to send adrenaline surging up her spine.

She forced her steps to stay even, glancing back and around as if drinking in a last view of the picturesque town. The car moved no faster than the posted 25 mile-per-hour limit, which was suspicious in and of itself. She spotted a park ahead, complete with walking trails, according to the wooden sign. She turned onto the drive, breaking into a speed walk as she stepped onto the wooded path. A moment later the SUV drew abreast, slowing as it pulled into the parking lot. The tinted windows told her nothing as she glanced back, but the heavy tactical gear on the woman who stepped out of the driver's seat was enough to set Nel running into the foothills. *Fuck, that is way too close.* There was no way to know if they had actually made her or just wanted to check. Terribly dyed hair was annoying enough in the mirror. In person it might be a dead give-away.

She wove through the trees, boots skidding on the loose pine needles and loam. An upraised root snagged her sole and she caught herself on the truck of a tree. Her palms ripped. The raw skin stung with bark, dirt and sap. Her heart hammered in her throat, rattling in her trembling body. Was that the pounding of her pulse or military-issue boots in her ears? She dragged herself upright, whirling. Which way had she come from? Suddenly all the trees looked the same, all the hills were identical. The trail was gone, splintered into game trails and imaginary paths her eyes picked out from desperation. Her legs shook, ankles giving out as she picked a direction. Every third step pitched her back toward the ground. The trees thinned at the crest of the ridge and she tucked herself behind one to scan the surrounding woods. Her bare skin, starving muscles, and exhausted mind were no match for tactical gear. Her gut decided it was the time to jettison the gas station hot dog, and she vomited in the bole of the roots until her stomach simply cramped around nothingness again. *This is a joke.* Her eyes burned, her throat ached, her hands stung. The buildings of the town were invisible behind the trees and hills, but over the hills came the sound of bells. *One. Two. Three. Four.* She would never make it, not if she stayed huddled at the base of a rotting tree. The woods were still, even the wind held its breath to listen with her. The sun was pendulous above the horizon and Nel forced herself to her feet, kicking leaves over her vomit. She turned her back on the haven of Bethleham and jogged into the hills.

6

Chattering stream water was music to Nel's ears. Between the crackling of the wires overhead and the buzz of cicadas in the trees, her head needed a break. Even the access road was overgrown in this area, and the last sign of people had been the deer blind. The ground rose steadily toward the rocky crest of the ridge. The river sounded just inside the tree line. She paused to catch her breath, hands braced on her knees.

"Woah." The ridge rose to her left. The ground fell away into a cleft along the side of the hill. The grassy corridor draped a gold necklace across the emerald throat of the valley ahead. She had been hiking for almost two weeks now, and the yellow tinge to the grasses and the nutrient-starved trees in the wetlands reminded her that the chill of fall was fast approaching. The river chattered down the slope of the hill and followed the cut in the rock where the corridor arced over the land.

Millennia of water wearing at the rock had carved a series of pools and tiny canyons. "This looks like some computer screen saver that I'll never find in real life." She stripped her clothes off and dunked them into the shallow eddy at her feet before laying them out on the sun warmed rocks.

She dipped a toe in. It was cold, but manageable, and nothing said she had to be filthy just because she was a fugitive. A yelp escaped from her throat as she hit the water. The pool was deceptively clear, and well over six feet in the center. She scrubbed at her hair, rubbing the fine sand from the edge into her hands and face to scrub the filth from her skin. Shivers shook her muscles and her fingers turned blue. Briar scratches slashed stark red against her goosebumped skin. Her stomach was a forgotten pit between her ribs. Bug bites and bruises peppered her body. *But this is the happiest I've felt in weeks.* She hauled herself up onto the rocks, blissful at the sun on her naked, battered body. The warm stone dug into her back pulling snaps and pops from her vertebra as she laid back. There were half a dozen reasons to keep moving, but her clothes were still wet, and the Institute had yet to give her a deadline. She allowed her eyes to close.

Burning pain and a cold wind woke her sometime after noon. Her skin was tight with sunburn. Half the scratches on her forearms and neck were now a series of bubbling welts. "I fucking hate poison ivy." She had been vigilant of the hairy, red vines and the evil-looking leaves. She hadn't been so careful during her haphazard dash through the woods outside of Bethlehem. The cold water had done wonders for her muscles, but most of that was countered by sleeping for several hours on rounded granite. Her stomach gurgled and she shoved herself up. What was left of the second hotdog was still stowed in her pack, and she carefully cut off one inch before wrapping it up again. It had to last as long as she could make it, and as far as she could tell it had yet to spoil, despite several days in her pack. Guilt and shame ate at her for puking up the only food she had seen in weeks. *Might as well have eaten the two dollars and saved myself the trouble.*

The sky muttered from several miles away and she glanced up. Clotted blue clouds gathered over the next hill, causing the chill that had woken her. *Rain. Of course it's going to rain.* The clothes on the grass were still damp and cold, but she pulled them on over her goose-bumped skin. Her ankle was more swollen than before, and she had to re-lace her boot to force it to fit. She crossed her fingers that the inflammation and press of steel-toed leather wouldn't cut the feeling from her toes. As much as she wanted to, she knew better than to soak her foot in the cold stream running down the hill. Swelling was a natural cast, and she couldn't afford to re-injure herself.

Another survey of her body distracted her. Her muscles still hummed from running and various aches told her where bruises would soon appear, if they hadn't already. She hauled herself to her feet and tottered to the stream. She finger-combed her too-bright hair and splashed water onto her face before applying mud to her poison ivy. Even if it didn't actually help, it cooled the itching.

When she powered up the phone to check her messages the battery icon in the corner was blinking. *Fuck.* She hadn't thought this far ahead. She hadn't really thought at all. The fluctuation between the summer-hot sun and the chill of the night was doing nothing to help the phone hold a charge. She was unwilling to make a foray into another town, but her one connection to the outside world might force her to reconsider. The corridor was narrower here, one of the lines branching off to the southeast a few miles back. The poles were the newer metal ones, broad and an odd blend of futuristic and ancient, as if some alien culture had forgotten them millennia ago. She snorted. *No, when the aliens visited then, they were too busy being philanthropic abductors to mess with the infrastructure of our power grid.*

The clouds gnashed their teeth again, this time closer. A moment later, rain hissed against the gravel. Nel lowered her head and trudged on.

7

Noon heat hung heavily over the corridor. Nel was desperate enough to consider flicking on her phone, but each time her thumb paused on the button she told herself to wait just one more minute. The phone's battery was dangerously low, and she had limited herself to only turning it on every other day at noon. She rounded the bend and froze in the overgrown trail. *Fuck.* A cluster of half a dozen people watched her crest the rise, brows furrowed with as much confusion as concern. She could have blamed her preoccupation with the phone, or the 85 blistering degrees, or even the steady itch of poison ivy burning its way up her left calf. She would have been lying. There was nothing to blame, but her own complacency.

She pulled her bandana further down under the guise of wiping sweat from her brow. "Hey, guys." Her attention bounced from the garish orange safety vests to the cluster of upright shovels and discarded Stoney Knoll screens. One half of her wanted to shriek with relief at finding her own people. The other crawled into a knot of dread. If anyone had their finger to the pulse of the case, it'd be archaeologists. Most looked startled, but she didn't see glimmers of recognition on their faces. *Yet.* "Sorry, didn't mean to sneak up on you."

"Thought you were a bear, honestly." A tall woman stood, shoving a tangle of tight black curls back into her bun. Deep purple had replaced the pink streak in her forelock, but Annie's eyes were still luminous against the deep brown of her skin.

Nel's jaw clenched, her legs prepared for flight. *There's no way she doesn't know what's going on.* Annie's gaze flitted from Nel's battered appearance to the miles of deserted trail behind her. Nel watched the pieces tumble into place behind Annie's calculating frown. Finally, her mouth curled and she grinned. "Been a while, yeah. Gang, this is Liz, she's an environmental surveyor, hence why she looks shittier than we do right now." Annie's eyes bored into Nel's, daring her to spoil the hastily cobbled cover.

"At least I'm avoiding that lovely shade of neon."

Annie snorted. "And you'll be the first to get shot by a hunter. You going to be in town for a while?"

"Not too long."

Annie fumbled a card from her pocket and scribbled on the back with sharpie. "If you're free give me a ring. We can grab dinner or something, if you're in the area."

Nel shot her a wan smile. "Been busy, but I'll see what I can do." She waved at the rest of the crew, avoiding eye contact as much as was socially inconspicuous. "Nice to meet you guys, good luck!" She hoisted her pack and continued down the trail, forcing her steps into steady strength. Perhaps they wouldn't watch her leave. Perhaps her falsely springing steps would convince them she hadn't been hiking for three weeks.

♠

Nel glared at the vultures circling above the corridor. "I'm not dead yet, you fuckers." She paused on the top of the ridge to watch the field vehicles. The two Tacomas bounced over the rocks and turned out of the access road. Nel tried not to wish she could run after them, begging for a ride. For the second time since she ran, Nel contemplated turning herself in. If she wasn't the murderer, then she would go free. The trial would be complicated and frustrating, and a heartbreaking trip down a section of memory lane she would rather avoid, but she wouldn't be starving and covered in poison ivy. *But what if I am the murderer?*

Another glance at the vultures told her they weren't, in fact, being terribly preemptive about her fate. Instead, they were more interested in something tucked into a dense thicket of saplings. She hauled herself up the rock face running between the two lines of structures. A mess of blood and entrails decorated the grass. The fat corpse of a three-point buck stretched on the ground in the thicket. The smell was sickening, a mix of too sweet blood and rancid rot. Her stomach twisted, but try as she might, she couldn't say it wasn't partly out of hunger. *There was that article about how you could eat rotting steak as long as you scraped the nasty parts away. Or mold?* Part of her knew that a violent bout of food poisoning would do nothing to help, but another part, the louder, hungrier one, told her that if she didn't eat, she would be dead in a week.

"Ugh, all right." She slung her pack off and dug through the pockets. Her trowel wasn't nearly sharp enough to cut through raw meat. Her small pair of root snips were in the bottom, covered in several years worth of dirt. She took a deep breath, held it, and crouched next to the deer. The meat was slimy and grey on the outside, the sun warming the fat enough to make it greasy. Most had been scavenged by coyotes, judging by the prints and teeth marks. One leg was missing, as was most of the throat region. She shoved the body over onto its other side and almost vomited as a writhing wad of maggots fell from somewhere in the belly. She cut away a flap of skin and snipped a softball chunk of meat out of the more protected flank.

She backed away, dragging her pack away with her foot, before inspecting the meat. It was mostly pink, though the edges had faded to brown in spots. It smelled, but she wasn't certain if it was the meat itself of the echo of the rotting corpse behind her. She needed to find water and a campsite before she brought it anywhere near her digestive tract. She wrapped the meat into an old plastic artifact bag and tucked it away with her clippers. The corridor rounded a hill, and in the distance she could see a valley that might boast a stream. *Hopefully one without pollution and orange slime.* Sure enough, half an hour later she slid down the bank of a river. It was deep and clear, if silty. She rinsed her hands, grinding sand into her palms to scrub away what bacteria she could. She dunked her head in, relishing the icy ache of the cold water as she gulped until her stomach burned. The water bottle was next, and she held it upstream from the sediment her drinking kicked up.

There were fewer trees along the rocky section of corridor, but a copse tucked beside a wetland looked dry and secluded enough for a camp. A quick scouting trip produced dead wood and enough dry grass for tinder. She set up her camp and a small shelter before returning to the stream to clean her clippers and the meat. Tempted to scrub it with sand too, she scraped the edge of her trowel against the greying areas until most of the slime was gone. "I really hope I don't regret this."

"Ten bucks says you will. No pun intended."

The fire was slow to start, and the damp wood smoked horribly until it dried enough to truly burn. When the flames were smoldering enough, she held the end of a stick into the coals until she could sharpen it against a rock. With the meat impaled and perched above the sullen fire, she could finally sit back. She tugged Annie's card from her pocket. The logo was unfamiliar, but the name was one she had heard in passing at a few local conferences.

Annie Jones, Crew Lead

Public Archaeology Of Northeastern U.S.

Nel grinned. She'd done well with Annie, regardless of Mikey's assessment and concerns. She'd miss the woman, but she knew Annie would do as well with another advisor as with her. *She'll be all right, despite her time with me.* The meat spat angrily, dropping globs of grease into the already spitting fire.

"Or perhaps because of it."

8

Nel woke to the sensation of something sharp twisting high in her gut. Her eyes flew open and she shoved herself upright. However well she had cooked the meat, it hadn't done the trick. She staggered into the bushes and was violently ill. When her stomach seemed satisfied with its emptiness she slumped back onto her makeshift bed. It wasn't over, she was sure, but for now the pain subsided.

"Fuck." The next twelve hours were going to suck, if they didn't kill her. She glanced at the fire. It was just a bed of coals, glowing far more cheerily than the fire that birthed them had burned. She drank what was left in her water bottle, but that seemed to only reawaken her food poisoning.

After the third bout of vomiting, she crawled back to the fire and fished her phone from her pack. She pressed the power button, hands trembling from weakness and adrenaline. The phone trilled itself awake. She squinted against the blindingly bright screen. 11:51. She hastily dialed the number, restarting twice when her cold fingers fumbled over the buttons. Three rings and a breathless answer.

"Hello?"

"Hey, Annie, it's Liz. From today."

"Oh! Right." Fabric scratched deafeningly across the mouthpiece as Annie excused herself from what sounded like a normal round of dirty beers. A door clicked shut. "Hey, we can talk now."

"I'd really rather not over the phone."

"How are you doing?"

Annie's soft tone wormed into the anxious shell Nel wove around her heart every morning. She swallowed hard. Should couldn't bring herself to answer. "Are you in a hotel?"

"Nope, working locally. Got my own place."

"Is that where you are now?"

"No, I'm at a friend's. Are you in trouble? I mean, more than, you know...." Her silence was too gentle to be awkward.

"I don't know." Nel's eyes burned, her throat swelling her words into choked growls. "I haven't showered in two weeks, I'm covered in poison ivy, my ankle's twisted. I found a dead deer.... I think I have food poisoning. I hadn't eaten since the day it rained." She drew a shuddering breath. "I don't even know what day it is."

"Are you still on the right-of-way?" Annie's voice hummed low across the crackling phone line.

"Yeah. Made it until dusk before I got too dizzy to walk."

"What was the last structure you passed?"

"132, I think."

"Sanders Lane crosses the corridor about a fifteen minute walk to the north. I'll meet you there in twenty."

Nel forced herself up and gathered her things. She counted her steps until she faltered somewhere between 38 and 44 when she stopped to be sick again. She almost stopped on a low ridge, but the dim grey line of the asphalt against the black of the underbrush in the distance pushed her on. The ground sloped steeply up to the edge of the road. Somewhere water sputtered from a culvert. She slumped against the hill, eyes unfocused on where headlights would appear. It was cold, even for autumn, and she pulled her arms out of their sleeves and into her shirt. She was too deeply entrenched in the safety of her mind, her swirling almost-dream thoughts, to hear the crunch of gravel under tires, or the pad of running shoes on the access road.

"Shit." Annie's voice was low, her hands cool on Nel's sunburned cheeks. "Come on, let's get you out of here." She hauled Nel into her arms, carrying her up the last few meters of access road. The car was still running, hazards winking into the faint mist rising from a nearby wetland. Annie bundled Nel into the passenger seat, tossing her pack into the trunk a few moments later.

When Nel finally opened her eyes, the heat was blasting and Annie had just pulled into the middle lane on Interstate 93. Annie wordlessly handed her a full water bottle.

"You could be arrested for this."

"And you could be dead."

Nel looked away, watching the lights fly past her window. "Thank you."

"We'll be home in ten. You can stay for as long as you need."

"Just a night, maybe two."

"I wondered where you were, what the hell you were doing. Half the time I worried they had already caught you, only to get new bulletins for your arrest."

"Yeah, I've been lucky."

"What the hell happened last summer?"

Nel shook her head. "I don't know where to begin."

"I guess I wouldn't either."

"You do CRM now?"

"Yeah. Since I'm done with classes I figured I could get some experience while I work on my thesis. That group was mine. I'm a crew chief now with PANEUS. I took your advice about switching from academia."

Nel swung her head back to look at Annie's profile. Gorham's lights silhouetted the warm brown of her skin with sporadic starbursts. "I'd probably be dead tomorrow if you hadn't come. Thank you."

Annie smiled faintly. "You would have done the same." She took an exit onto a state highway.

Nel looked away. She wasn't certain she would have. She stayed silent until Annie pulled down an overgrown dirt road that led to a little A-frame.

"This yours?"

"Yeah, I rent it from the people who own that big house at the top of this road. Been here a month, and so far so good. It's peaceful, you know?"

Nel hummed in response and stumbled from the car. She followed Annie through the door. The apartment was clean, decorated with turquoise and purple. Posters from the last Summer Olympics hung in the living room.

"Bathroom's through there. I'll get you some clothes."

Nel moved slowly across the room, one hand supporting herself on the wall as she went. The bath room was tiny, with a narrow shower stall. Now that she was surrounded by the cacophony of Annie's shampoo and coconut oil, Nel realized exactly how bad she smelled. "Fuck, Bently, you're gross," she muttered to herself.

Annie ducked her head in. "Towels are in the cabinet, same with wash clothes. Use whatever shampoo and soap you want."

"Thanks."

"Stop saying that, Dr. Bently." When Nel looked up, Annie smiled. "You'll wear it out."

Nel's laugh was closer to a cough. When the door shut she cranked the hot water and stripped out of her filthy clothes. The apartment had an old shower head, one that banged and sputtered before spewing stinging droplets. Nel stepped in and tilted her head back. *I could die right now and be happy. This is bliss.* It took three washes before she felt anywhere close to clean. Her hair left rusty rivers down her bruised skin. She emerged after what must have been close to half an hour. The room was filled with steam. She wiped the mirror clear then wished she hadn't. At some point between the second and third wash, Annie had left a stack of pajamas on the toilet lid. They were loose, made for someone of Annie's tall, muscled build, but they were clean, and Nel didn't even care that bright turquoise clashed with the safety-orange of her hair. She padded out into the living room. Annie had pulled out the sofa-bed and was busy tucking sheets in. She glanced up and her brows arched. "Wow. The new hair is...cheerful."

Nel rolled her eyes. "Don't start. Let's see how good you look as a fugitive."

Annie chuckled, but her smile faded after a second. "I know it's complicated, but can you give me something? I'm happy to let you stay here, but I'd like to know what I'm getting into. As much as you can tell me, that is."

"Fair enough." Nel slumped onto the pull out and tucked her legs underneath herself. "Things got so fucked up. I don't even know where I'm running, or why, half the time. It doesn't make me look innocent."

"What happened? One day we had a baller site and were finding all sorts of cool stuff. Then Mikey's dead and we're sent home. Now there are more bodies."

"Bodies?"

"They found another two days ago."

"Fuck."

Annie picked at the loose threads of the afghan blanket. "Nel, are you guilty?"

"Not of murder." She looked away. "But the person who probably is guilty, is out of town. The Founders were so much bigger than I thought, and our benefactors were a whole other mess." She cleared her throat over the sudden lump that must have been from being sick. "Right now I can barely think straight."

"But you were there."

"Yeah. I was. I still can't make sense of it."

When Nel offered nothing more, Annie rose. "I'll let you sleep."

"When do you work tomorrow?"

"Tomorrow's Saturday. I'll be home all weekend. We can talk more then, and figure out a plan." She smiled, pushing her curls away. "Sleep well, all right? You're safe here."

Nel climbed under the covers and turned away. The light flicked out. The night was quiet, the breeze outside did not tug at Nel's hair or drag heat from her body. Instead, she was warm and tucked between three soft pillows. *Safe.*

9

"Hey." The bed shifted as Annie sat in the crook of Nel's knees. "You awake?"

Nel kept her eyes closed, her breath even. She wasn't ready to face the world just yet. After a moment, the weight behind her legs disappeared and the front door opened then closed.

"She's just trying to help you. Stop being sorry for yourself."

"I'm a fucking fugitive. I think I've earned the right." She blinked and stretched. He was right. Rather, whatever part of her subconscious choosing to use her dead best friend's voice was right. She slid out of bed, wincing at the pounding in her head. After a woozy moment she closed the sofa-bed and tottered into the kitchen. Annie had scribbled a note on the counter.

Headed into town. Got a few errands to run. Grabbing you some stuff, so you better be here when I get back. Coffee's

*in the press, just pop in a pot to heat it
up. Sorry there's no microwave!*

<3 A

Nel rolled her eyes at the heart and tugged open the refrigerator. The milk was thankfully new, and she set about reheating the coffee. Annie had left the computer on and logged-in. It took Nel just a moment to pull up the Google Earth images of New England. She zoomed in until she found the corridors she had traversed. They were mostly deserted, sweeping north east. At some point she would have to cut through the woods if she wanted to make it to the border. She hadn't thought this far ahead. She hadn't thought half this far. She assumed the Institute would fetch her at some point. The whole do-our-dirty-work-for-us litany was growing stale. *These will never do. I need details. I need to know where the houses are, where the roads are.* Her gaze turned to Annie's field pack. She needed real maps. As desperate as she was, she could wait until Annie returned to ask. It wouldn't do to piss off her only real ally so far. She had finished two cups of coffee and was looking up Los Cerros Esperando VII when she heard tires in the drive. *About time. I'm going nuts boxed up in here.* She moved to the door, but froze.

Three silhouettes loomed in the tiny curtained window, and none of them that of the buxom field tech. The knock was all business. *Who knocks on their own door?*

"Annie Jones?"

The knock sounded again. "This is the police. We just need to ask you some questions."

Nel caught a glimpse of a suit and tie through the crack in the curtains. She shoved her fist in her mouth and pressed herself to the wall. Annie had sprung for a nice apartment with lots of southern exposure. And lots of windows.

"Annie Jones!" The knocks turned rough.

"There's no car in the lot, sir."

"Let's take a look around."

She listened as the boots moved off the stoop and crunched through the gravel of the drip line around the house's exterior. As soon as the shadows were gone from the door, she bolted for the bathroom. Its window was covered in peeling privacy etching. She slipped behind the shower's curtain and curled up in the bottom. It wouldn't fool them if they entered the house, but she doubted they had a search warrant. She resisted the urge to press her hands over her ears. Instead, she bit down on her bare knee, ignoring the ache as her teeth dug into the layers of bruised flesh.

"Do you think that kid just wanted attention?" The voice was right under the bathroom window.

"I dunno. Tossing his boss under the bus is a bold move." The second voice was that of a woman. One of the officers tested the window. Nel's breath hitched in her throat, her heart hammering until the window proved locked. "We can come back."

Several minutes passed as they moved about the exterior of the house, Nel listening as they tried the sliding doors and a few more windows before returning to their cruisers. After a moment the vehicle ground out of the driveway. Apparently they had more pressing matters than to camp at a young woman's apartment.

The bathroom was dark and cold. Her legs fell asleep and her butt cramped. Nel couldn't bring herself to move. *That was far too close for comfort.* She watched the sun sink behind the trees through the top of the window. Her mind wandered down every dark road her brain produced. She had not allowed herself to think beyond her next step, her next move. The furthest she planned ahead was where she might sleep that night. Now, frozen with fear with only her thoughts for company, every concern rose to the fore. *I haven't even called my Mom.* She couldn't, she knew. Not safely. The cops would undoubtedly be watching her house, listening in on her mother's phone. It was the longest she had gone without talking to her mom in years. Even in Chile she found time at least once a week to check in.

Hot tears inched down her cheek and she bit her lip to quiet her hitching breath. If there was ever a time to want her mom, this was it.

The front door banged open. She stifled a yelp with her fist again, shivering from cold and fear as she pressed herself against the tub, as if she could somehow merge with the cold porcelain.

"Nel?"

She shuddered, swallowing past her fear. She tried to uncurl her legs, but burning tingles raced up her skin. "Here." Her voice came out a faint croak.

"Nel? You in the bathroom?"

"Come in."

The half-open door swung open and Annie peered around the shower curtain. "Fuck, what's wrong?" She crouched beside the tub and wrapped an arm around Nel's shoulder. "What were you doing?"

Nel allowed Annie to help her up, stumbling over the lip of the shower and into the brightly lit hall. "Sorry. Didn't mean to scare you." She swallowed. "Cops stopped by the house and I panicked. They were looking in the windows. Figured they wouldn't see me there."

"Shit." Annie ran a hand through her dense curls. "Sit on the couch, all right? I'll get you something to drink."

Nel did as she was ordered. She tucked her legs under herself and leaned back against the cushions. Her heart was still rattling around in her chest. "There were two cops and they had some dude in a suit with them. They did a circuit of the place outside and knocked a few times. Said they were from the police department and just wanted to ask you some questions. They mentioned that some kid had tipped them off. They wondered if it was for attention, but it sounded like it was one of your employees."

Annie pressed a beer into Nel's hand and flopped onto the other end of the couch. "This is a nightmare."

"You don't fucking say." Nel rubbed her face roughly. "You have someone looking to get you into trouble?"

"Not that I know about. They might think I'm the one in trouble, that you might come after me, or force me to help you."

"Right."

"When was this?"

"They came by around ten maybe?"

"Christ, you've been in the bathtub since then?"

"I was worried they might come back. I couldn't leave, with you getting me supplies. Then my legs were asleep." She looked down. She had just begun to relax. Finding Annie was a relief. She didn't expect so many strings to get tangled up. "This has gotten way bigger than I thought."

"Well, I mean, international murder hunt. It probably just feels big."

Nel shook her head. She appreciated Annie's optimism, but knew better. *This is way bigger than that.* "Some stuff happened this summer. Shitty stuff. Beyond Mikey's death."

"Does this have to do with Los Pobladores? Or the black stuff we found on the site?"

Nel's eyes flicked to Annie's. The secret was burning in her chest, igniting her tongue every time she opened her mouth with the need to get the knowledge outside of herself. She couldn't tell her there had been rocket fuel under sediments that were several thousand years old. She couldn't tell her who Lin really was, or what Los Pobladores were hiding. "Yeah. The site was more important than we realized. It goes way back, and it's important to more than just Los Pobladores. There's another group, the people funding the dig, and they want this stuff, this history out in the open. Mikey and I got caught in the crossfire of a Stone Age war." She shrugged. "I wish I could explain it more, but I don't know much more than that. I don't even understand half of what happened, what I saw."

"Nel?" Annie's eyes were dark, unreadable, and fixed on some point out of the window miles away. "Were we on the wrong side?"

Nel's breath shuddered from her lungs. "I don't know. I still could be, but I'm in too deep to go back now."

♠

"Here." Annie overturned her bags on the floor, plopping onto the carpet to dig through her haul. "C'mon, I've got a ton of stuff that'll help you. You were too shaken earlier for me to show you." She reached over and pulled Nel onto the ground beside her. "The gumbo will be ready by the time we're done and we can get crazy and have dinner to go with the beer."

Nel snorted, but she could tell the mirth fell short of her eyes.

Annie's brows curled with concern. "You all right?"

"I'm on the run from the law and the only place I've actually been able to sleep was buzzed by the cops." She pulled her hand free, reluctant to let the comfort go. Though the police hadn't returned, she was still jumpy. "Show me what you've got."

"First aid, including sutures—had to go to three stores to find that one—a canteen and iodine tablets, space blanket, socks, feldsnaptha, bug repellant, and a ton of these MREs and just-add-water things."

Her chest was suddenly tight. She had assumed she was entirely alone without Mikey. "You're the best. Despite all my efforts to be a shitty teacher it seems I at least made an impression."

"Nonsense, I'm just worried you can still fail me retroactively." Annie's full lips curved into a sudden smile. "So I know you're committed to doom, gloom, and anger, but I doubt the cops will show up tonight. You any good at video games? I've had a hankering for Battlefront II, but the computer's no challenge."

Nel answered her grin with one of her own. "You're looking at the woman who got 'Deadeye' every time." She shoved herself off the floor. "You get the game set up, I'll plate the food."

"You're my guest."

"And you also cooked and I kind of owe you a lot." She scooted into the kitchen and set about finding utensils and plates. She poured them both another drink before balancing everything and returning to the den. Annie was crouched in front of the television, clearly playing find-the-disc-I-put-in-the-wrong-case. Nel paused in the doorway, tilting her head. Annie's gym shorts were a horrible shade of green, but her brown legs were thick and muscled. Nel shook herself and deposited the drinks and plates. *Stay cool, Nel. She's too young for you. And probably doesn't swing your way.* She slumped onto the rug and started a single-player campaign while Annie dug into her meal.

"I seriously hate being one of the heroes in this. I prefer the normal way of doing things."

"Cause being a robot with a blaster is normal."

"Hey, no judging there, missy." Nel laughed and paused the game to enter in a cheat.

"What the hell was that?"

"Now we're invincible."

"We're on different teams. We'll be perpetually shooting at one another."

"Yeah, well I needed another beer. Fire away, Annie." Nel snagged another bottle from the fridge, then went back and grabbed what was left of the twelve-pack. "Here. I figured these weren't long for the world."

"Not at all." Annie popped the top off one and took a few deep sips before glancing at Nel. "I'm glad you called me. This is fun."

"Yeah. I'm glad you believe me."

"You might be able to bury someone and make it look like we were never there, but I don't really think you're capable of murder."

Nel looked away. She was. In the heat of the moment—literally, considering the shed was on fire—she had stabbed someone. Whether it was a killing blow or not, it didn't matter. It could have been. *I don't even know his name.*

"What happened down there?"

"I really don't know. I mean, I know the events, I saw everything unfold. But I can't really say I know what the hell was going on."

Annie looked away, apparently content to let Nel have her secrets. "I'm really sorry about Mikey."

"Yeah, me too. I didn't mean to get all doomy again." Her smile was sheepish. "I'll be right back." She went into the kitchen, pressing the sweating side of her bottle to her brow. The den was too hot, and her body was aching and tingling. She recognized the impending threat of a bad decision. The Formica cooled her cheek when she laid her head on the countertop. The sounds of laser blasts echoed from the other room for a minute, then faded into silence as Nel's mind drifted. Alcohol muffled everything, swaddling her in warmth and comfort.

Warm hands skimmed up her sides, hard fingers kneading the knots from around her spine. Nel hummed appreciatively, eyes sliding shut as she arched her back into the massage. "Archie hands are the best."

"You can say that again." Annie's thumbs rubbed tiny circles under Nel's shoulder blades. Her voice was low, as rough as her work-worn hands, but slid like honey over

Nel's ears. She pushed Nel's shirt up and over her head. Her movements were unhurried, but insistent. Nel pulled the shirt the rest of the way off and tossed it aside, grateful that she hadn't bothered to put her bra back on. After weeks of worrying and planning, she was ready to surrender. Her hum of pleasure turned into a moan when Annie's fingers dug into the twisted muscles of her sacrum.

When her hands dipped under the waistband of her pants, however, Nel's eyes flew open. "Whoa, wait a minute." She turned around, bracing herself against the counter while the world spun into place before her eyes. "We can't do this, Annie. You're my student."

"Not anymore."

"You're a kid."

"Ew, no. I'm twenty-seven. You're what, thirty?"

"Thirty-five."

"Still, not even ten years." Annie moved closer, planting her arms on either side of Nel. "I'm fine if you don't want to, I'm not going to turn you in or anything."

Nel grimaced. She hadn't even considered the blackmailing. "That's not what I'm worried about. This just feels wrong." She couldn't help but tilt her head, eyes lidded as Annie's breath ghosted over her throat. "That's why I want it so much."

Annie giggled. "You must be drunk to say stuff like that."

Nel rolled her eyes and glared at her. "I'm serious, though."

"So am I. I'm a grown woman and you are no longer my advisor." She pressed her hips against Nel's. "So unless I don't get your engine revving, I see no reason why we shouldn't enjoy ourselves."

Nel drew a breath, dropping her willpower in a pile with her pajama pants. "Do you mind finishing what your hands were doing? My body been through hell the past two weeks."

Annie motioned with her finger for Nel to turn around again. Her mouth dropped a kiss at the nape of Nel's neck. "Can I call you Dr. Bently when we fuck?"

"Fuck, no." The second word trailed into a low moan, however, and Nel hung her head. This was bliss. She muttered incoherent rebuke when Annie's hands left her for a moment. They returned a moment later, working tension from Nel's scratched legs. Her fingers worked upwards again, and slid between Nel's slightly spread thighs. Nel shifted, letting her chest rest against the counter top. Annie's fingers were gentler now, but hadn't ceased their rhythm. Instead of knotted muscles, now they teased tension from the tight tendons around her center, thumb sweeping from clit to lips and back before moving back out to tamer territory.

Annie shifted, and before Nel could ask why, the other woman's tongue was following her fingers' path. Her tongue traced fire across Nel's skin, swirling between her dense blond curls. She gasped as two fingers slid into her. Pleasure burned inside as Annie's tongue mirrored the rhythm of her hand and Nel's ragged breath. Nel's fist slammed onto the island as she came, wetness pooling around Annie's curling fingers. She shuddered, letting the sensation crash over her. She found her legs unable to support her and she dropped to her knees, clinging to the counter top.

Annie slid her arms around Nel's waist from behind her, trailing wet kisses up her shoulder. "Come to bed."

"I came right here."

Annie snorted at the bad joke and tugged Nel's limp hand. "Doesn't mean you can't again."

Nel turned, capturing the girl's dark lips with hers. Beer made Annie's full mouth cold for a moment before it melted into liquid heat under Nel's kiss. Nel followed the younger woman down the hall and into bed, her eyes still misted from lust and the trance of cold-hot kisses. Of all the ways to go on the run, she decided, fucking her way north was probably the most original.

18

"You need another check-point though. This fugitive thing is hot and all, but no one's going to know if you break an ankle or get eaten by a bear."

"Fuck that. I don't have a ton of friends, you know. I only did the CRM circuit a few times, never for too long at one place. Besides, I fucked my way out of most friendships."

"OK, well, any amiable exes?"

Nel looked down at the living room floor, still strewn with survival supplies and beer bottles. Apparently her habit of leaving in the morning was coming back to bite her in the ass. "There's this one ex I have. She's always done right by me, by everyone, really. She might be available. She was supposed to be somewhere up north finishing her thesis this fall."

"You have her number?"

Nel rattled it off. Other than Mikey's and her mom's it was the only one she ever bothered to memorize. She stared at the phone Annie handed to her. The number was dialed and the line already ringing. Nel glared. "Thanks for giving me a chance to compose myself."

"Hello?"

Nel fumbled the phone up to her ear and stammered out a greeting. "Hey, um, hi Tabby."

"Nel?"

"Yeah." Nel turned away, tracing the pattern of the rug with one socked foot. She heard the sliding door shut behind her and silently thanked Annie for understanding. "What're you up to?"

"Fucking really? I'm not that far out of the loop. Where are you? Are you safe? What the hell is going on?"

"Yeah, I'm safe. I actually was calling for a favor."

"I figured."

Nel winced, but didn't argue with the pointed barb. Tabby was honest to a fault, which wasn't a problem, except for Nel. "Yeah. I'm headed north, and I was curious if you'd gotten to rent that place you were looking at."

"Yeah I did. Been here a month. You need a crash-pad?"

Nel snorted at the porno reference. "Seems like. Just for a night, just to get my bearings and thaw out. Nights are getting cold." She listened to the silence on the other end. She could almost hear Tabby's kindness warring with her logic, with the various scars Nel had left scattered across her heart. She knew kindness would win. With Tabby it always did. "Look, I'm not aiming for—"

"Stop right there. I'll give you a place to crash, but I've got too much to focus on without rehashing our multiple failed attempts at romance."

"I'm pretty sure it was my failure anyways." Nel almost grinned at the shock that must have crossed Tabby's face. "Anyways, where about are you?"

"Magalloway, on a lake. How were you planning on traveling?"

"Hadn't gotten that far. I've been going under the radar so far, but already ran into some old friends. Thankfully I haven't burned all my bridges just yet, and I was able to stay with one of my old students."

"Corridors?" Tabby asked.

"Yeah, how'd you know?"

"It's what I'd do. The corridors are miles away. And I wouldn't trust the roads. Everyone knows everyone else round here and you'd be caught within an hour. How are you with water?"

Nel shrugged then realized Tabby couldn't see her. "Um, fine, I guess? I can swim, if that's what you mean."

"Nel, I'm not going to tell you to swim a hundred miles." Rustling papers echoed across the line for a moment. "You have access to a canoe or kayak?"

Nel glanced at the large shed on the edge of the yard, just visible through the sliders. "I can check. If nothing else I'll pay Annie and she'll buy one. You thinking I could row up?"

"Yeah. This house has a bunch of hiking and boating maps. I'll find some way to send you a picture. I assume the cops have broken into all your social media accounts."

"It's a fair bet." Nel snapped her fingers as a thought rose in her mind. "Do you still use your uni-email?"

"Not much, but the password still works. You want me to use that?"

"Yeah. Make sure it works, then send a text to the number I called you on."

"Sounds good, Nel." Silence hung in the air for a moment, then Tabby cleared her throat. "I'll text you."

Nel shifted. This was worse than seeing one another in person. There, at least, she'd be able to comment on Tabby's newest hair color or piercing. "You're a lifesaver, Tabby. Literally. I'll text you when I'm headed up."

"Stay safe."

Nel glanced up as Annie stepped back into the room. "Hey, quick question, you know where I could get a canoe or something?"

"I take it your conversation went well." Annie's black brows drew together as she processed Nel's question. "Wait, you're not seriously thinking of paddling to Tabby's are you?"

"Well, it's kind of a brilliant idea."

"So she came up with it?" Annie sighed. "Yeah, there's a kayak in my landlord's shed. Said I could use it whenever."

"Will he need it anytime soon?" Nel leaned against the wall, hiding her shaking hands behind her back. Her emotions were tattered, stretched too thin between the cops the day before and talking to Tabby for the first time since the funeral.

"You planning on capsizing or something?"

"No, but then, I didn't really plan to be framed for murder."

"Right. Sorry." Annie looked away, running one hand through her tousled mass of curls. "I'm just worried. You leave here and I'll never know you made it, not unless you get caught or your name's cleared."

"Well, let's all hope for the latter, OK?" Nel jerked her head at the shed in the rear of the property. "I assume the stuff's in there?" When Annie nodded, Nel sank into the couch. "And where's the nearest place to put in? Tabby's sending me some maps and stuff today."

Annie blanched. "To your email? Are you fucking crazy? The cops have got to be crawling all over your laptop by now."

"No." Nel glared at her. "She's sending them to herself via her old uni email and I'm logging into her account."

"Wow, she's trusting. I doubt I'd ever give anyone my password. Even someone as good in bed as you."

Nel snorted. "Well, lucky for me Tabby is the most trusting human I've ever met, except for..." She stopped and swallowed. "Wanna check out the kayak for me? I'm still freaked by those people who stopped by, and I don't trust your neighbors not to blab if they see a stranger in your yard."

"Well they'll start to wonder if I have someone chained in the basement, after the noise we made last night." She rose and stepped out onto the back porch. "I'll haul out anything you could use, k?"

"K. I'm going to see if she emailed yet." Nel watched Annie jog down to the shed. *What are you doing, Bently? Impromptu sabbatical or not, she's your student. Grief sex with the people who fund you is bad enough. But this? You're way beyond desperate.* She wanted to tell Annie the truth about the site, about everything that happened that summer, but a nagging voice told her that it wasn't Annie that she really wanted to tell, but anyone, someone who would listen, who wouldn't send her packing to an asylum. *Someone whose career wouldn't be ruined by association.* Outside, Annie was dragging a pink kayak onto the lawn, face screwed up in disgust at the number of spiders or earwigs crawling through the sun-bleached plastic.

Nel shook her head with a faint smile and typed the college web address into the computer. Sure enough, Annie's phone lit up with a text.

KLINET@POTSDAM.EDU. PASSWORD IS STARCROSSED27

Nel grinned. *Starcrossed, eh?* As an undergrad, Tabby had a dramatic streak. With maturity it turned into confidence and attitude, both of which Nel appreciated. The loyalty, though, had been too much at the time. She opened the first email, one without a subject line. Sure enough, three grainy pictures were attached. The last had a red circle around a large lake, and an "X" on the eastern shore. Tabby's handwriting was still spiky: *Home*

"Hey, I think I've got everything you'll need." Annie leaned on the door frame. "Did you get what you needed?"

Nel nodded. "Printing them out now. Your printer has paper, yeah?"

"I think." Annie peered into the dusty machine under the desk. "Enough. When did you want to leave?"

Nel shrugged. "Never. Yesterday."

Annie grinned. "I feel like that's how you always feel at another woman's house." She jerked her head at the bedroom. "Let's gather your things and get you packed. I'll drop you off at dawn tomorrow."

Nel shook her head. "I think it should be tonight. I know it's crazy, but I just can't stop moving. Those guys really got to me, I guess."

"It's dark at night."

"Thank you, Lord Captain of the Obvious."
Nel tugged the dark maps off the printer and
peered at them. Her route was clear, but
upstream. *Time to have the arm workout of this
little fugitive-fun-time.* "But I know what you
mean. I'll be fine. You got me that headlamp if
anything really serious happens. I've been
hiking during the night too, when I couldn't
sleep. Water won't make it much different."

Annie shuddered. "Just creepy is all. I
guess I'll load things onto the car, then."

Nel watched her go. There was a sickening
weight in her chest. She slipped into the bed
room and dumped her bag out. Instead of
making her feel in control, this time, it was
overwhelming. *How can I survive with just
these things?* She had survived for weeks with
less, and she knew the panic would look
different from the other side, tomorrow. The
various supplies Annie had procured were
already tightly rolled and tucked into a plastic
bag. Her bag was bulging, her borrowed
clothes baggy around her smaller frame. *I look
about as ready as a man headed for the gallows.*
She sincerely hoped it would never come to
that.

The front door banged and Nel slipped into
the kitchen. The process of leaving wasn't easy

for anyone, and she would rather face it alone until absolutely necessary. A large Tupperware sat on the counter. It held the last of the pirogues and pizza, as well as some plastic-wrapped iodine packets, to keep them extra dry. She tucked it into her bag and snagged another water bottle from the fridge. The house was quiet. It was the strange grey light between day and night that was too bright for lamps, and too dark to really see anything clearly. Nel brushed the counter where their sex began the night before.

"No one knows how to make a disaster as perfectly as you."

"You've given me a run for my money." The screen door banged shut behind her as she slipped outside. She tossed her bag into the car's back seat, watching Annie in the side mirror as she tethered the kayak into place on her roof rack.

There was a reluctance in the dark woman's movements. Annie finally slid into the driver seat. Her hand rested on the keys, but didn't turn them. "Nel...."

"I'm ready." She looked away, at some distant, unseen point, but let Annie's hand brush hers on the way to shift the car into drive.

She hoisted the kayak off the rack, shaking her head when Nel tried to help. "You'll be doing this enough. There are two portages on your way north." When Nel shot her a curious look, Annie shrugged. "I checked out your maps while you were in the bathroom washing up. I wanted to know where to look if you didn't make it."

Nel stared, even though Annie refused to meet her eyes. She was suddenly scared. More scared than when Los Pobladores destroyed her site. More scared than when she saw Lin's brother descend from a flying saucer. She recognized the sinking feeling in her gut, the whirling of her thoughts.

Annie's hard hands on her shoulders jolted her out of the cyclone in her mind. "Hey. Sorry. You'll be all right. You're the strongest woman I know." Her full lips quirked. "Maybe text me when you get there?"

"What if the cops take your phone? I can't risk that."

"Right. I know." Annie steadied the kayak and motioned for Nel to climb in. "C'mon, you've got the law on your tail, Bonnie, and they won't stop just because you wanted to get one last barbed comment in."

Nel smiled and slid herself into the rubber-edged seat. The paddle was awkward at first, but she managed to shove off from the shore. She double-checked that her bag was secure and raised her hand. She had left dozens of women, waving as she slipped from their lives into the dusk of anger and fear. She had refused to text them for as many reasons as there had been lovers. She had never looked back, and she didn't now, but she felt the weight of Annie's eyes on her shoulders long after the sky was fully dark.

Someday, she promised herself, someday she would emerge from the chaos of her own mind and someone would be standing on the shore, hand raised in welcome. Sometimes, even, when she was lonely, she imagined the features of that woman's face. She still didn't know.

11

The river meandered, mostly wide and calm, curling between gently rounded banks that looked as if they had been the same for centuries, though Nel knew they probably changed with each season. The corridor had been a lesson in greens and blues, the rolling vista of the power lines dipping into the purple hills. The river was different. She was wrapped in brown of the banks and the black of the water. The trees curling in overhead were dark brown and tan, their leaves flaming crimson as they died.

As the only child of older parents, Nel was often alone. She spent hours in the woods and fields surrounding her family's farm house in Springfield. The adventure and possibility in that solitude had done a lot to mold her independence. Now, alone and in the woods, again, it was far different. The nights were growing longer, and the crisp smell of autumn was the bitter bite of winter. She bent into the paddle and propelled herself through a calm swath of dark water. It was a narrow part of the river, deep and carved into the dense brown silt of the banks. Her archaeologist's eyes traced the layers of sediment, the map of the river's history laid bare. Often erosion of river banks exposed sites, points and bones and middens spilling from between the centuries of soil.

"There's got to be a site up there."

Nel glanced up at the high bank on the right. Large pines clustered at the precarious edge, the boles of their trunks larger than her arms could probably reach. "For sure." Another day she would have drawn up at the bank and scanned the strata for artifacts while Mikey walked over the top and sifted through the exposed roots of toppled trees. *Not anymore.* She shook her head and bent into her paddling. When she watched her feet on the corridor, avoiding poison ivy and bees and a dozen other hazards, her mind was occupied. Now she only had to keep eyes out for other kayakers and rocks beneath the surface, or the odd bear. She found herself speaking aloud more and more, loosing track of how many times she imagined Mikey's responses. "If I ever get out of this, I'll sound like a nut job."

"When did 'when I get out' turn into 'if'?"

She sighed and shook her head, ignoring the thought while she watched a great blue heron, black against the pink of the dusk sky, wing its stately way to some distant wetland over the hill. She would have to find a place to shore up soon. Tomorrow, if her mental record of where she passed was correct, would bring long swaths of fields on either side, and she was determined to cross them in one go. People didn't much care if someone camped on a river bank in the woods. A farmer's livelihood, however, was not something she was willing to mess with. Around the next bend was a long gravel strand tucked in the curve of the water. A loamy, pine-covered terrace sat just above it. The plastic of the kayak hissed against the gravel and she lurched out of the craft and onto land. Her legs trembled, worse than any sea legs she had experienced. She dragged the kayak fully onto land and unclipped her bag. The light was still bright enough for her to keep her footing as she clambered up the bank. "There's totally a site here too."

Her first night on the river two days ago, she discovered a small tarp tightly rolled in her space blanket and tied with several meters of thin cord. As much as Annie claimed to be a city-mouse, she knew her camping gear. Two trees provided the posts to string the rope between, and she draped the tarp over it. It wasn't the fanciest thing, but it kept out the worst of the wind and rain. A foray down to the strand gave her cobbles to weigh down the edges. She wished she had a sleeping bag, but Annie was a strict blow-up-mattress-only camper.

The thick layer of pine needles meant no fire, but the night was still warm enough that Nel only missed the comfort and not the warmth. She leaned against the tree just outside her tent and pulled out her crumpled maps. She had passed under a power line corridor early in the morning, and through a wetland to the west of a small housing development from the seventies. Traveling by water was far faster than she had imagined, and with each obvious landmark, she ticked off another section of the river on her crumpled map.

She found the development and the series of tight curves that had followed. She drew a line through the river where she thought she might be camping and circled some banks that promised to be good sites. "When I'm done with this fugitive gig I'll come back here. Maybe phone up the state archaeologist and get him to do some field schools up here."

"You don't want to run them yourself?"

"Yes, because parents love entrusting their kids to someone who ran from the law. I doubt I'll be teaching after this."

"You don't sound as sad about that as before."

"Well, at this rate I'll be lucky to survive the next few months without incarceration." She tucked the maps away and changed into her long pants and shirt to watch the sunset. The sound of the river was more soothing than the tiny faux-rock fountain Martos had in his office. It was like the murmur of conversation in a cafe, both lonely and comforting at once. She was tempted to turn on her phone, but knew better than to waste the battery. The hot sun on the river cooked the technology and she didn't trust the charge to last until she reach Tabby's despite how fast she might be traveling. Leaving her cell in her car was a good choice, but part of her wished for the distraction from reality while the light faded from the sky.

"A distraction from being a fugitive or from seeing Tabby?"

"Which one do you think? Seeing Tabby is scarier." She hadn't seen the other woman in years, at least, until Mikey's funeral, and even then they had barely spoken. Tabby grabbed her hand, hugged her, but that was it. Before that Mikey and Nel had gone to help Tabby on a site where the archaeologists had gone missing. *And she'd been with that cop woman.* Nel had been with more women than she could really remember, but there had only been a few that had gotten under her skin. That had stayed in a corner of her heart even after Nel left. Tabby was one. *And so was Lin.*

Tabby was scary because Nel knew she would be there no matter what, knew that if Nel asked, she'd do anything. Nel saw that as a weakness. Even now, some part of her scoffed at the idea. But she understood it more now. Lin—no, not even. Lin's employer—told her to run. And she had. Granted, running was something Nel was good at. *So why does it scare me this time? Aside from the fugitive nonsense.* Why did she feel like, for the first time, she was running towards someone, that she was the one who would be heartbroken? Nel was struck with sudden sympathy for the women whose hearts she had broken.

The clouds turned from orange to red and finally to purple. The stars blinked into brightness as the day withdrew. Only in Chile was the starlight so clear. Nel stared at them, reciting in a whisper the few constellation names she remembered, and making up new ones for those she didn't.

"You said you missed me, Lin. So come find me." *You see that blue star? Somewhere between here and there.*

♦

Nel slid the paddle into the river. The current made the water feel thick against the lacquered wood. The river was broad and smooth. The trees closed in above her head, the overgrown banks bore marks of several floods. She itched to pull up on the strand and look through the exposed strats for artifacts. Instead, she propelled herself further north. On the river she was just another dirty hiker, a crunchy backpacker with poorly dyed hair.

I'm so out of my element. She paddled close to an overhanging tree where the river split. Her map was grubby and half dissolved from splashing, but Annie's clear handwriting highlighted each fork. This river would take her toward Magalloway. *And Tabby.* Nel hated drama, especially her own. She hoped Tabby would realize only life-or-death would bring Nel crawling back to her door. The river was choppy, the walls narrowing, granite jostling her from bank to bank as she moved upriver. *Of course they wouldn't send me somewhere downriver.*

The water curled eastward and the tree dropped away as she entered an open area that was half-lake, half swamp. A few doublewides were backed up against the water to the west. Nel cut east to the tiny cabin perched high on the eastern bank with a view of the wetland. She had no idea what to say, how to broach the subject—any subject, really. The lights glimmered in the dusk light, and she pulled out onto the muck-laden beach. She stumbled twice as she pulled the canoe out of the water and fumbled with her backpack. The cabin's three-season walls muffled a big dog's excited greeting. Finally Nel looked up. A stocky, athletic figure was silhouetted against one glass door to the patio. Nel raised a shaking hand.

12

Warmth and the smell of wood smoke billowed from the house as Tabby ground the sliding door open. The brown, shaggy dog let out a series of excited yelps and mutters. "Settle, Indie." Tabby tugged him aside to let Nel in. Her eyes never left Nel's face.

Nel shut the door and slid the lock into place. "Hey."

"Hey." Tabby fiddled with her blue tuft of hair.

Nel dropped her bag as close to the door as possible and toed her boots off before easing herself onto the couch. "Sorry to show up like this."

"You look like death."

"Love you, too."

Tabby's pierced eyebrow quirked. "Now you say it."

"Don't be a bitch."

"You're stuck with me regardless, you know. Being a fugitive and all." Her hand brushed over the scratches on Nel's cheek. "Run out of your first aid things?"

"Didn't bring one. Annie gave me some, but I wanted to save it for the big stuff."

"You're more stupid than I thought."

Nel reared back, summoning the dregs of her spirit to glare at the other woman. "Didn't have a whole lot of time to plan, what with running from the law and all." She slumped against the couch. "I had some stuff left over from the field season, but my main kit's at home. I was going to replenish it."

"Well, I've got one." She rose and offered Nel her hand. "C'mon. Let's get you cleaned up."

Nel allowed her to pull her to her feet and followed her into the bathroom. Her brows arched at the Jacuzzi tub and huge shower. "Quite the place you've got here."

"Not mine. I'm renting while I finish my thesis. Figured I'd be away from distractions up here."

Nel winced, as much from the accusation as from the ache in her shoulders when she tugged off her shirt. "If I didn't have Lyme's before, I'm betting I do now."

"Is that some thinly veiled come-on?"

"Yeah," Nel sneered. "Fugitive's don't have Netflix, so I've resorted to 'Tick-check and Chill.'"

"Shut up and get out of that nasty stuff. You smell like a bog body. Before the preservation."

"Thanks." Nel stripped, piling her clothes in the corner by the hamper. She perched on the edge of the tub, suppressing a shiver. The porcelain was cold and her bones ached.

"Rinse off. I'll get some coffee going and then draw you a bath, all right?"

Nel stepped into the bath and turned the water on. She waited to close the drain until the water ran clear, rather than the brown of dirt and dried blood. She toed the drain shut and leaned back, not bothering to wait. Scalding heat seared her skin and stung the scratches on her legs and arms. Still, she was certain this was heaven. The door slid open and she opened one eye. "Hey."

"Hey." Tabby sat cross-legged on the broad shelf of the tub surround. Two steaming mugs sat next to her. "I brought some bubble bath and coffee."

"Thank you." Nel closed her eyes. "You don't have to sit with me."

"I don't mind. Besides, it's not like I've never seen it."

"Aren't you with that cop girl? Jessica?"

"Jennifer. And no."

"Oh." Nel dunked her head under the water, giving herself time to think. She was never tactful. She scraped her hair back and surfaced. "I thought you'd get back together."

"Hard to get back together when you were sleeping with me."

Nel opened her eyes. "Takes two to tango, sugar." She regretted the words immediately. She didn't want to fight. "Sorry. I've been alone for a bit. It's not easy to remember how to talk with humans."

"You were never great at it anyways." Tabby's smile softened the words.

"That was Mikey's deal." She leaned back. "I never got a chance to thank you for coming. To the funeral, I mean. It meant a lot to his parents."

"I didn't do it for them."

"I know." Her throat was suddenly tight and the heat seemed to press on her chest, making it hard to breathe. She made a show of reading the bubble bath bottle, unable to meet the other woman's eyes. "You think you can find some clothes for me? I'm gonna soak a bit longer then I'll be out."

Tabby nodded and rose, taking her mug with her. "I'll be right outside if you need anything."

♠

Nel emerged from the bath, taking far longer to dry and dress than was strictly necessary. The cabin was what Nel had pictured for the vacation she and Mikey had always planned, though perhaps with more fake taxidermy. She could hear Tabby moving around in the kitchen. The open living area was bright, the lake now just a cavernous darkness somewhere off the porch. Indie lay on the couch, but his one good ear flopped upwards and he looked up at her.

She smiled and crawled onto the spot next to him. Talking to animals was always far easier than talking to actual people. She glanced at Tabby, whose back was to her. *Especially some people.* She rubbed under Indie's chin. "Did he come with the place, or is he yours?"

"Mine." Tabby smiled at her and held up the empty box of frozen pizza. "Hope you don't mind this for dinner."

"Not at all. When'd you get him?" Nel had always wanted a dog, but being away for weeks during the summer hadn't seemed fair. Now she was doubly glad. *Having a companion while on the run would be nice. I'm fine with me starving, but a dog?*

"He belonged to someone down in Starsboro, where I met Jen. His owner passed and Jen and her partners were on the case. I couldn't just leave him down there. Too many kill shelters and all that."

"She not a dog person?"

"She was living with friends at the time. Not sure how they or her cat, Jim, would feel about it."

Nel snorted. "Good name. I like people names for animals."

Tabby shifted, her faded college-era sweatpants skimming her full legs. "You all right?"

"Fine, yeah, why?"

Tabby's brow arched at the multiple answers. "You seem lost."

"Well—"

"No, I mean more than just the fugitive thing." She shot a curious glance through the oven window before perching on the ottoman across from Nel. Her strong arms folded across her knees and Nel had the sudden impression that she was about to have a therapy session.

"I'm just exhausted." Her hand traced a pattern across Indie's head. He didn't seem to mind. "Being here is perfect, and I'm grateful, but I can't pretend it's easy."

"Why isn't it? What's so complicated?"

Nel shrugged. "Us. We're complicated. As much as I used to pretend I'm a robot and can't feel human emotions, I can. And I feel like even by being here I'm taking advantage of your big heart. Again." She looked down. "And there's your cop to think about."

"I said we were over."

"Not from where I'm sitting." Nel smiled. "Whenever you mention her you get that look in your eye, the softness and light. You might not be dating, but you've still got the bug."

Tabby rolled her eyes. "She's a great woman, but things are complicated. Her job requires a lot out of her, and so does mine. It doesn't leave a lot of room for each other."

"Or yourselves." She sighed. "I've been so lost in work for so long, now that I don't have it I'm having trouble remembering who Nel is." She sighed. "And I have no idea what is happening out there. I can't check in on the case really. When I actually start thinking about a plan or Lin, or my mom I start to panic. No one runs from the law and makes it, Tabby. I keep having visions of this all ending at the edge of the cliff and suddenly I'm jumping."

"Except?" Tabby prodded.

"Except what?"

Tabby rolled her eyes. "You had a look. That one that you get when you think someone will run if you tell them the truth."

Nel looked down at the dog, at the floor, at her socked feet, anywhere but Tabby's face. "No, I don't."

"I spent a year staring at that look, hon, I know it better than I know my own face."

Nel swallowed hard. "That vision. On the cliff. I think I already jumped."

Tabby's hand was slow, but certain as it reached across the distance and took Nel's "I know. I think you did, too. Something happened this summer. At the funeral you were different. I thought it was Mikey's death, and maybe it was. But you've had the ground pulled out from under you. I know you haven't told anyone what happened down there, not really."

"I have. Mikey. A hundred times. Sometimes he even responds." Her hand flew to her mouth and she winced. That wasn't something she needed to tell anyone. If she wasn't already earning a ticket to an asylum, that would seal the deal.

Tabby didn't acknowledge the confession. "You can tell me. You know I'd take it to my grave." Guilt crossed her face. "Sorry. Bad cliché to choose."

"I know I can. When I make sense of it, I will. But it's weird. Weirder than I can explain. This world is fucked up."

Tabby snorted. "Yeah. You forget I've had a long year, too. Seeing the stuff Jen does for work, it makes me think twice about things. Three times sometimes." She winked and shoved herself off the ottoman. "C'mon, I think the pizza's burning."

13

Moonlight glimmered through the windows at the foot of the bed. Each time a cloud passed, the light flickered on the wall by Nel's head. She shivered and tugged the mossy-oak patterned comforter higher. Now the air was too still and she felt smothered. She tossed onto her other side. Tabby's back was to her, her shoulders moving evenly with her breath. They had crawled into the bed without touching, and even now the two inches of space between their pajama-covered bodies buzzed like uranium. Nel moved her hand as close to Tabby's hair as she could, hoping the other woman might feel the change in the air. "Are you awake?"

Tabby shifted and muttered.

Guess not. Nel tucked her arm under her head. "I'm scared, Tabby. I want to trust these people—they funded my work and seem to believe the same things I do, except, I don't know if they really do. The Institute is huge, they have fingers in pockets I don't even know exist. They have the kind of influence that you read about on conspiracy blogs. And their tech is out of this world. Literally. I want to help Lin, I want to help her bring light to humanity or whatever, but part of me can't trust that as the truth. I think she believes it, but she's so idealistic. And then there's that night in Chile."

"You mean the UFO sightings?"

Nel glanced over. "Did I wake you up?"

"A bit, but I don't mind."

"How much have you heard?"

"Conspiracy blogs." Tabby reached over and took Nel's hand. "I know we're not together, and I know we don't really fit that way, but I do love you and you're one of my closest friends. I think I know more about what happened down there than you realize."

Nel frowned. "I doubt it. What did you say about UFO sightings?"

"There was a rash of them down in Chile around the same time you were there, just a week before you got back, roughly. In the hills of some rural town. I didn't know where I recognized the name from until I realized it was the location of Los Cerros Esperando VII. You're talking about conspiracies, about big organizations and tech and bettering humanity. I think I've seen this movie." Her eyes were soft in the moonlight and she shifted to face Nel, as if they were middle-schoolers at a sleepover.

"I know it sounds crazy." Nel looked at her pillowcase, plucking at a loose thread.

"Yeah, a bit. You know what also sounds crazy? An evil god summoned by a dude to kill teenagers parking in cars. A creature taking the form of the person you love and breaking your heart just to feed off the despair and fear. What about all those archaeologists that went missing when we were on that site when you met Jen?"

"What are you talking about?" Despite what Nel had seen in the last few months, she was fairly certain Tabby was speaking nonsense.

"Nel, When I said Jen's work makes me think twice I wasn't talking about how shitty humans are to each other. She doesn't just work as a detective on those cases. Her partner studies things that can't be explained by human things, cases that don't fall into the realm of reality as most people understand it."

"You're saying she's Scully." Nel scoffed.

Tabby sighed. "I'm saying that I'll believe you if you tell me Lin works for some part of the government and that aliens are real."

Nel swallowed hard. "Yeah. They are real. She grew up on a spaceship filled with people descended from a culture that went missing 13,000 years ago. Her brother stopped by Los Cerros Esperando VII to check on her progress on saving the world. Didn't go as she wanted, though, so she's on probation." Nel's eyes flicked to Tabby's wide ones. "Believe me now?"

"If it were anyone else, I wouldn't. You're the woman who would rather read *Short History of Nearly Everything* than suspend your disbelief enough to watch *Roswell*."

"That was also far too much teen drama for my tastes. And to be fair, Bill Bryson does talk about extraterrestrial life." Nel rested her forehead on Tabby's shoulder. "Thank you for listening. I've been talking to myself for so long."

"Have you called your mom? I know you two were always close."

"I called her the day I ran. We were supposed to talk that afternoon. I can't, though. I'm sure she's been questioned. I'm sure she's found out what's going on."

"And I'm sure she doesn't give a fuck about that and is worried sick about you. It's been weeks, Nel. Almost a month. Call her."

"I can't, it's too late."

Tabby rolled over and flicked on the light. Nel blinked against the brightness. "What the hell are you doing?"

"It's nine-thirty in the evening on a Tuesday. You're calling your mom."

"This will tip them off big time."

"Nel, honey, you might be a fugitive, but you're no OJ and they certainly don't have the budget or the interest to tap your mom's phone. Besides," Tabby looked away, "I've been calling her every week."

"Did you tell her I was coming here?"

"No, I figured you could do that yourself. Besides, I didn't want to get her hopes up, just in case."

"In case what? I died? You dragged my body from the lake?"

"In case you changed your mind." Tabby fished the landline phone from its stand by the bed. "Here." At Nel's curious look she shrugged. "Signal's shitty around here."

Nel took the phone, thumb tracing the worn rubber buttons. "I don't know what to say."

"I'm sure she'll talk enough for the both of you." She tugged a pair of sweatpants on and nodded to the screened porch. "I'm going to take Indie out. Holler if you need me."

"Right." Nel waited for her to leave, and for the front door to thump shut. She waited another two minutes for good measure. Then she dialed.

The phone picked up after half a ring. "Tabitha? How're you doing?" Mindi's voice was low, almost raspy the way it used to get when she stayed up late if Nel was sick.

"Hey, Mom." Nel swallowed past the sudden tightness of her throat. She heard a door shut and the creak of her mother's favorite chair.

"Baby?"

"Yeah."

"I love you. Where are you? Are you all right?" Despite the tension in her words, Mindi kept her voice level.

"I love you too."

"Are you safe?"

"Yeah, for now." Nel shifted, tucking a pillow into her lap. "I'm at Tabby's. Just got here today."

"What's going on? I had cops here, and they're saying things, honey, things I can't believe."

"I can't really explain it. If I could, I wouldn't be here."

"Does this have to do with Mikey?"

"A bit, I guess. I'll explain it when I'm home." There was a pregnant pause, and Nel could feel her mother's pointed stare through the phone. She felt like she was late for curfew. *I am, I guess. By a few weeks.* "I don't know when it'll be, Mom, don't look at me like that, I can feel it from here."

There was a hitching noise that could have been a sob or a laugh. Perhaps it was both. "Oh honey, I can't even explain how worried I've been. I had to hope you were safe if they were still looking for you. But after Mikey, I was so scared, honey."

"Me too, Mom."

Mindi fell silent. "Are you all right? I mean, really?"

"I don't know. I'm warm now, and dry, and safe for a few days. And then I don't know. I have some people looking out for me, I guess, but half the time they cause as many issues as they solve. It's all I've got right now." She shrugged deeper into Tabby's shirt. "You haven't begged me to come home."

"I know better than that. Your dad raised you to be determined, but I'm where your fire came from. I know you're not a coward. You'll come home when you can."

Nel could hear the tremor, and knew the effort it took for her mother to say those words, to admit that her arms weren't the safest place for her daughter anymore. "I love you."

"I love you, too."

"I won't be able to text or call again for a while. I don't know when."

"I know. And the cops have been by every few days. I wouldn't trust another call, not from another line, at least." She paused. "You're with Tabby?"

"Yeah."

Her mother snorted. "I knew it. As much as you put that girl through Hell, I knew she'd help you out. It's too bad you're terrible for each other. She's the kind a mom dreams about."

"I'm a fugitive, Mom. Matchmaking really isn't something I'm concerned with." She swallowed again. The tightness had lessened, and her eyes were clear again. "Has Martos called?"

"Once, in the beginning. I don't think he knows what to believe. I can give him a message, though."

"No, it's all right. He's so fucking moral, I don't trust him not to think he's doing the right thing by turning me in, expecting it to be a lie and them to clear my name."

"Honey?"

"Yeah?"

"Is it? A lie, I mean." Mindi's voice was quieter, almost a whisper.

Nel shrugged, though it was to no one. "I think so."

"But you don't know."

She glanced out the cabin window at the engulfing blackness of the night and the dark water beyond. "I don't really know anything anymore."

"Honey, you know I love you, I will always love you. You have friends and allies. Go to the cops and talk everything out. I'm sure this can be fixed."

"I can't." *I've come too far now.* "There are others involved." She heard a sudden click then a faint buzz. She had watched too many political spy movies to trust that it wasn't a phone tap. "I think I ought to go. I'm exhausted."

"Please be safe. Please. I love you."

"I will. Tabby will keep you updated as much as she can. And I'll call again when I get the chance."

"I don't want to hang up. I don't want to say—"

"It's not goodbye, Mom. I'll be fine. We'll get this figured out." She swallowed hard and hung up before her mother could hear the shaking in her voice.

When Tabby returned, Nel was still sitting on the coverlet, the phone crouched before her. "Are you alright?"

"No." Nel could feel the weakness threatening to overtake her.

Tabby set the phone aside and rested her forehead against Nel's. "Can you trust me?"

"Of course."

"Then let me do the thinking for you, for once. Just close your eyes. Exist." Tabby moved closer until every possible inch of their bodies was pressed to the other's. Her hands moved slowly, running up Nel's back, through her hair, down her throat. Her mouth followed, more intimate than seductive. Tabby's fingers slipped under the waistline of Nel's borrowed pajama pants. They had been lovers long enough that she knew exactly how to move her thumb, curl her fingers. When she came, Nel felt tears on her cheeks, tasted the salt as she gasped against Tabby's lips. She shuddered, curling into the other woman's arms.

"It's OK to jump, Nel." Tabby's fingers laced with Nel's. "I'll catch you."

♠

Nel rose at dawn. Tabby was gone, and so was Indie. Remembering her almost-religious morning runs, Nel glanced at the bed-side clock. She had twenty minutes before Tabby returned. Her clothes were still warm from the dryer. She dragged on as many layers as possible and shoved the leftover pizzas into the vacated space in her bag. She logged onto the computer and brought up Google Maps.

Her finger traced the river, found the lake, and followed the road north. There were fifteen miles of wilderness to the nearest corridor, but it arced northeast, like a beacon pointing to her goal. After snapping a picture with her phone, she deleted the search history and shut the computer down. She glanced at the clock. Fifteen minutes.

She found a pack of sticky notes by the phone and wrote two lines:

Thank you.

I'm sorry.

She slipped out the rear door. The opposite shore of the lake disappeared in the mist, and the tops of the pine hills were cloaked in fog. It was silent, save for the chilled chirps of a few birds at the bear-battered feeder. Two deer paused to watch Nel as she moved across the driveway and toward the woods. By the time she heard Tabby's sneakers pounding on the gravel of the long driveway, Nel was jogging through the trees towards the Northern Lights Corridor and Canada.

14

That evening it started to snow. Not the fat flakes that heralded times with family and skiing. Instead they were the tiny, driving crystals that were closer to ice than actual snow. They hissed against the dry leaves and coated everything with a hard, cold dusting. Nel swore and flipped her hood up. She hadn't planned on snow. She hadn't planned on being on the corridors for so long, or not finding Lin or the others yet. *I didn't plan on any of this.* Her boot slipped on the snow-dusted leaves as she clambered up a hill. Her legs went out from under her, and her hands scrabbled at the half-frozen rocks. Her chin smacked on a piece of ledge jutting from the road.

She screamed, a roar of anger that petered into frantic laughter. This was ridiculous. She was willing to hike through the woods for these people. She wasn't willing to die. "You want me, you sick bastards? Come and fucking get me!" Her fingers were too numb to text without a dozen typos, but she still flicked the phone open and pecked angrily at the keyboard.

FUCK YOU. FUCK YOU ALL. YOU WANT ME TO SHOW UP AT YOUR DAMNED BASE? SEND A CAR AND WE'LL TALK.

It may have been impulsive, but she was done. She was finally tired of fighting, tired of screaming into the void of her life and only hearing silence back. She slumped against the structure, pulling her legs up to her chest. A different kind of anger bloomed in her heart, something cold and searching.

"Hey, She-Hulk. Remember to breathe. Stand your ground, but remember to breathe."

"You gonna tell me not to be so angry?"

"No, not yet. This is just the beginning, and sometimes rage is the only thing that burns bright enough to carry you through. Remember what the trick is?"

"Yeah. I'm always angry." Her shivering moved deeper until it felt like even her organs were shuddering from the cold. "Mikey, I love you."

"Don't start with the doom talk. Trust me. They'll come for you. I know I would."

"Yeah, well you're not fucking here, all right!" The flakes tapped across her upturned face. The structure loomed overhead, black against a grey sky. She rested her head on the cold metal and wished she believed in prayer.

She spent the next four hours walking off-and-on. When her body grew too tired and she stumbled more than stepped, she would find a structure and rest. When her eyes lidded and her muscles seemed too warm for the weather, she forced herself up and continued to walk. By noon, the sun was still firmly tucked into its dismal, grey blankets. The snow had turned into the slow, soaking rain that drenched the soul as much as the skin. She staggered to a stop under a pine tree. Her feet were two unfeeling blocks, and her fingers burned from cold.

She pried her boot laces loose, peeling her socks from her clammy flesh. Her toes were hard, white knobs. She rubbed them harder, but could only feel the base of the last three. *Fuck.* She hadn't considered frostbite before. She knew to keep herself warm but her impromptu drenching had thrown every precaution out the window. She glanced at the maps. She wasn't close, not even by a little, and the clouds to the south boded ill for any chance at getting dry. She wrung her socks out and tucked them into her pack, before tugging on a dry pair. Her boots were wet, but she couldn't do anything about it now. Her blanket rolled up nicely and she strapped it across the top of her bag. A few minutes combing through her wet hair and wiping dirt from her face made her at least feel more presentable. *If I'm going to do this, I'll do it right.* Finally satisfied, she shouldered her things and limped onto the road. She moved north, refusing to allow herself to rest. Wheels hummed on the rough tarmac in the distance and Nel turned to face the northbound car, mittened thumb extended. She plastered a tired smile on to her face. Hitchhiking was one of her worse ideas, but it would keep her from freezing to death.

After two hundred and seven she lost track of how many cars ignored her, or glared as they passed. At 9:23 a Peterbilt roared past, almost bowling her into the ditch. The J-break hammered in the cold air and the truck ground to an abrupt stop on the edge of the road. Nel forced her exhausted limbs into a jog and stopped outside the passenger door. The window squeaked down.

Instead of a portly, bearded man, there was a middle-aged woman, about as weathered as the mud-flaps of her truck. "Hey there, where you headed?"

"Oromoncto."

"Christ, woman, you'll freeze before you make it a mile. Hop in. I'll take you as far as Fredericton, long as you help me unload there. It's just under six hours."

"Deal." Nel clambered into the cab. "Thanks so much for stopping."

"I did my share of hitching when I was your age. That was forty years ago. World's not what it was then. I suppose you know that, though." She flashed a bright grin. "I'm Jean, by the way."

Nel caught herself a moment before offering her real name. "Lena." Her hand gripped the hard plastic of her phone in the inner pocket of her borrowed coat. "I'm headed up to visit a high school friend, but my wallet was stolen on the bus up from Bangor."

"Ugh, man, people, I tell you." Jean shook her head. "I've learned more than my fair share driving truck. Most of it good, but it feels like the nasty folk in the world are single-handedly trying to make up for all the good." She glanced over. "You want the heat on?"

"Please, I got drenched."

"I bet. And another storm's rolling in too. Glad I happened by."

"What're you hauling?"

"Frozen food for a truck stop of all things. The one just outside of Freddy." She glanced over. "You look exhausted. I've got my radio. You can take a nap if you need to. No worries about keeping me entertained."

Nel smiled. She was ready to protest that she was fine, but the heat sank into her skin, drawing every sleepless night to the surface again. She allowed herself to doze, mind spinning from the rattle of rain on the windows to the crackling duel of the FM and CB radios.

♠

"This is breaking news. Fugitive in the Chilean murder case, Annalise Bently has allegedly been spotted headed north towards the Canadian border just two days ago. A month ago a woman matching her description was seen hiking northbound along the TransCanada and Northern Lights power line corridors, but until now there has been no sign of the suspect."

Nel straightened as Jean turned the volume up.

The older woman glanced over with a sheepish smile. "Sorry, I'm curious."

"No worries." Nel almost scoffed as the radio went on with its theories. Still, adrenaline fired up her limbs. She forced her knee to still it's bouncing, and heaved what she hoped was a casual sigh. *Should I mention it? What if she's not really listening? What if it draws her attention to the story? If I don't mention it, will I look worse?*

"It is believed that Bently has disguised herself and is seeking a safe house with her former colleague, Dr. Nicolaas Van Riel, professor of paleovirology. Drivers should be wary of single people along rural northbound roads and hikers, hunters, and homeowners are urged not to approach strangers. It is not known whether she is armed, but she should be considered dangerous and unpredictable."

Nel rolled her eyes. She and Nico hated each other.

"What a story, eh?" Jean's eyes were fixed on the road.

"Yeah. You never know, I guess." Nel stared through the windshield, her eyes flitting to the faded reflection of Jean's face in the rearview mirror.

"This isn't an easy world to be a woman. The way I figure, a smart woman like her kills a guy, maybe she was doing the world a service."

Chills crawled up Nel's arms. "What do you mean?"

"I've been on the road for a long time. I've seen plenty of sick bastards get away with shit." Jean glanced over, her eyes far too steady for Nel's liking.

Nel crossed her fingers in her lap and played dumb. "That why you picked me up? You were worried I'd get attacked?"

"Partly. Mostly it was because orange really isn't your color." She jerked her sharp chin at Nel's hair. "You should have gone darker."

Nel's heart clawed its way past her throat and into her mouth where it fluttered on her tongue, smothering anything she could think of to say. *She fucking knows.* Jean seemed to think murder was retaliation to an assault, and Nel wasn't about to correct her. "The world really isn't easy."

"I won't tell." Jean's thick hands tightened on the steering wheel. "I picked up a college student headed home and that's my story. I'll drop you wherever you need to be."

"How'd you know?"

"Other than the bad dye job? The look on your face is far from innocent. You're haunted and that's for sure. I just hope whatever cloud is following you isn't from that guy you offed. You've gotta let that go, hon, or it'll eat you alive."

Nel picked at the calluses on her hands. They were already peeling after several weeks out of the field. "Why, though?"

"It's easier, sometimes, to just take it, but you know, after a while that anger builds up and we just can't take it anymore. We've got to fight back sometime." Jean shrugged. "And I get that."

Nel stared out the window, watching the undulating landscape. *Anger.* She was tired of the bullshit in the world, that was certain. And maybe, just maybe, Lin could help her fight.

♠

The All-Nighter was everything Nel imagined a Canadian truck stop to be: Tim Horton's separated by a normal convenience store from the greasy diner at the other end. The rumble of diesel engines was like distant waves. *And the parking lot is wet enough to be an ocean.* Nel slid down from the seat as Jean rumbled to a stop in one of the long parking spots.

"I'm going to pop into the store. You want anything?"

"Just some Gatorade. I can help you unload after, though."

Jean laughed. "With that face? Truckers listen to the radio, and so do the people in places like this. You'd best keep to yourself." She jerked her head at the pumps where two Mounties stood at their car. "Besides, we've got bored cavalry out tonight."

Nel stepped back behind the cab and shot Jean a smile. "Noted." She watched Jean disappear into the Timmy Ho's, then hoisted herself back into the truck to stay dry. She powered on her phone, but no new messages appeared. When she looked up again, one of the Mounties was headed towards the truck, flashlight out and one hand raised against the sleet. *Fuck this.* She cracked the door open and slid out, rounding the truck as he did the same. She kept the hulking trailer between them and jogged towards the wetland at the edge of the parking lot. Another five minutes and she was lost between the wet, black trunks of the trees.

♠

The phone trilled for the third time. Nel set side her last granola bar and grabbed the phone. "Oh for fuck's sake." There had been no signal for most of the past three days, and the moments she had any bars showing the Institute had been silent. The insistent box flashed across the screen.

BATTERY AT 5%

"Shit." She shoved the rest of the granola in her mouth and opened her messages. Still nothing. Between turning the phone on twice a day and constantly searching for a signal, it was a miracle the battery had lasted this long.

She opened her conversation—if it could be called that—with Lin.

PHONE DYING, BUT I'M CLOSE. IT'S A BIT COLD.

She copied the text and sent it to the Institute as well. It started to snow again. She wished she had stayed with Jean. She could have hidden, crawled into the back of the cab until the Mountie left. In the throes of panic she had forgotten how to trust anyone.

BATTERY AT 3%

She left it on for another minute, ignoring her still-rumbling stomach, but the envelope icon remained unchanged, despite the rare two bars of service. It chirped once, to remind her to plug in the charger, which seemed more snarky a reminder than usual. Then the screen when black. *Well, Bently, you're on your own now.*

15

Nel couldn't bring herself to stand. She had spent most of the night walking, knowing if she stopped, she would fall asleep and never wake up. Now though, she sat at the base of a tree just off Route 2. Cold wormed into her bones, into her foggy daydreams. It burned away the pain of bruises and sprains, leaving faint warmth in its wake. Her bleary eyes fluttered open and she peered around her.

Everything was covered in a thick layer of frost. White curls decorated the fallen tree that created a sheltered windfall. Nel had given up only twice in her life. All right, perhaps more than twice, perhaps a thousand times if one counted all the books she had put down and never returned to, if one counted the parties she had left before dawn, or the scattered hearts she slipped away from in the early hours when their owners were still sleeping. The second time was right before the SATs. She decided that college was a tool for The Man and that she didn't need a computer to spit out a number based on her arbitrary skills. She took every S.A.T. book that she had spent the past year pouring over and dumped them all into the backyard, doused them with gasoline and torched them. When her mom came to see why there was a bonfire in the backyard, she found seventeen-year-old Nel drunk, not for the first time, and proudly proclaiming that she would be damned if she was going to become a "cog in the machine."

The first time, though, that Nel remembered giving up, was when she was fourteen. The silence of the woods was agonizing, but far better than the infuriating chatter of their family living room during her father's wake. She had run into the woods, down the path that was so overgrown since her childhood that she barely recognized it through the tears. Her feet remembered, though. Sitting in the branches that once held her tree house, and now held rotted plywood, she gave up.

Her mother was shattered after Jerry's death, and Nel saw. She saw what love did, the aftermath of loss and the terrible emptiness that followed. The ripping left a hole, one with ragged edges that no one else would ever perfectly fit again. She gave up on ever letting another person take up that much space in her heart.

And until Mikey, she had succeeded. She hadn't thought a friend could be so close, or become family. She hadn't thought she would lose him at thirty-three. She wanted someone to reach out to, someone to hear her, to listen to all the complicated thoughts whirling through her head.

"You can make it."

"I can't. My feet are too numb." She glanced at the map she had hastily copied from her phone when the battery had started to go. The truck stop was just outside Fredericton off of Route 2. Her numb finger traced the grey line of highway on the map. *It'll take me two days if I only stop for a few hours.* She didn't have two days, not with her feet in their current condition. She laid in the frost on the ground now, toes numb with frostbite, body turning warm as sleep threatened to settle over her. And, just once more, she considered giving up.

"Up. Now."

Her body shook. Skin scraped from her palms as she grabbed at the tree trunk to haul herself up. "I can't."

"No. I can't. You can. You have to. For me. For you. For whomever you fucking want. But you can, and because you're you, that means you will."

She shook the worst of the condensation from her space blanket before folding it twice and wrapping it into a vest.

"This is the epitome of style, right here."

"Well, if archaeology doesn't work out for you, you can go into fugitive fashion."

She snorted and shouldered her pack. "Well, if death doesn't work out for you, come back, you fucker." She swept her tiny camp again and headed east. Her muscles protested at the movement, but warming them now was better than sitting in the cold. The air was still thick with mist, moisture rising from the wetlands like the Earth's breath. She wrapped her head and face with her scarf until only her eyes showed. She wished she had more foot-warmers, but she couldn't waste them during the day.

It was close to noon when she heard the low murmur of voices. At first she just thought it was Mikey, his imagined voice more real as the cold sunk deeper into her mind. A whistle pierced the tree trunks.

"Ahead. I see movement."

"Is it her?"

Nel glanced back. Two figures jogged through the trees. Their black tactical gear blended into the dark, drenched bark. She broke into a run, whimpering at the sharp pain in her toes. Her feet were leaden weights at the end of her legs, and it seemed that every few paces ended in a stumble. She moved closer to the highway. A break in the trees ahead brought with it the sound of rushing water. *A culvert or a bridge. It lost them once.* She hoped they hadn't learned their lesson. Then the ground fell away before her. Her momentum carried her over the edge of the ravine. Her pack cushioned the first landing, but not the second. She yelped as she broke through the thin ice and plummeted into icy darkness. The river was shallow, but filled with thick mud. She gagged on the gritty water and thrust herself to the surface. Rough hands grabbed her by the back of her coat and hauled her free.

16

She blinked water from her stinging eyes. Two figures in tactical gear flanked her. A familiar black SUV idled just off the overpass fifteen meters above them. A man picked his way down the slope. He wore a black wool trench coat over his suit. He spoke into a pin on his lapel. "We've got Bently. We're bringing her in."

"Fuck you! I'm fucking innocent! If you spent the amount of money you waste on S.W.A.T. shit on doing actual investigations you wouldn't be arresting the wrong people!"

"She's resisting," the Suit muttered into his lapel. "Yes, ma'am." He jerked a nod at the two men holding Nel out of the water. "Let's go."

"Sorry, Bently, you're coming with us."

Nel recognized the voice of the woman from Annie's house. "Fuck you, I'm not going anywhere!" She jerked her arm away and punched upward, grinning at the sheer luck as the woman's jaws clacked together.

"All right, you're done." The man jabbed cold prongs into Nel's kidney. Pain erupted up her back and down her limbs, and she heard the water evaporate from her clothes with a sizzle. She tried to jump, but her body wouldn't obey. Instead, she pitched back into the water, muscles seizing. Acrid water mixed with blood from the chunk of cheek she bit. The two tactical people pulled her from the water for the second time and dragged her to the bank. She couldn't even force herself to fight as the man hauled her up into a fireman's carry. Two Denali's were parked in the access road. Save for the strip of flashing lights across one windshield, they were unmarked. Nel fought the urge to vomit as she was bundled into the back of one. Reinforced glass isolated her from the two tactical officers. As much as she wanted to berate them with every curse she knew, her tongue would not move.

Nel expected gleaming steel gates, rolls of razor wire. She imagined stark white walls made for muffling terrible sounds. Wherever they brought her was a disappointment. The first gate they stopped at looked better suited to a junk yard. Moss and rust warred across the cold metal. The guard peered through the passenger window and the glass barrier at Nel before nodded and motioning them through. They drove for another fifteen minutes down a road that deserved an award for the most potholes ever.

The second gate was more what Nel expected. This time they were ushered into a gleaming hanger. Nel straightened, wincing at all the new aches caused by the taser. "Fuck." Wherever she was, it did not look official. The man knocked on the glass, presumably to wake her up, then rolled the barrier down a crack. "We're here. You gonna behave or do I have to hit you again?"

"I'm good." Nel croaked. "Where's here? I do have a few rights left, you know." The barrier was already closed. She sighed and ran her fingers through her mud-caked hair. If she had ever wanted to make a good impression, that hope was long gone.

Her door opened and The Suit held out a hand. "Come on, we've got to have a talk."

"I hate that phrase."

His manicured brows rose. "Well, I'm not breaking up with you."

Nel frowned. It wasn't like captors to joke. Unless it was at her expense. "Right. Arresting me is so much better." She slid from the seat, catching herself on the door when she staggered, rather than his hand. She wasn't willing to give him the satisfaction.

"If we were going to arrest you, Dr. Bently, we would have done it by now." The Suit motioned for her to follow him. "I'll take you to the medical wing. When you're checked out and cleaned up, then we'll sit down and explain everything."

"Ooh I love surprises," Nel sneered.

"Ouch. We were warned that you weren't armed, except for your tongue." He steered her down a brightly lit hallway to a pair of double glass doors. By the steel seams around the edges, Nel guessed they could be locked down in case of an emergency. *Or an escape.* As much as she pretended, she wasn't nearly badass enough to break out of whatever high security Snark Central this was. She limped after him, pausing every few steps to allow the pain to subside. The industrial-grade heaters in Jean's truck were amazing, but now that some feeling had returned, her feet were in agony. "You said I'm going to see a doctor?"

"Of course." The man shot her a vague smile that twisted Nel's gut. He unlocked a door to a large exam room and jerked a thumb inside. "Wait here. Someone will be with you in a moment."

Nel sank onto the bench, wincing when she heard the tumblers click into place as he locked her in. A johnny was folded on the exam table, but she wasn't about to willingly strip. She removed her jacket and hung it on the hook by the door. A tiny sink stood in one corner with some locked cabinets. She rinsed the worst of the dirt from her hands and face. She had moved on to finger combing mud from her hair when someone knocked.

"Come in."

A doctor peered in, clearly half expecting her to be waiting on the other side with a scalpel. "Dr. Bently?"

"Yeah." She returned to the bench.

"What's troubling you?"

"What's troubling me? Fuck, I've been hiking for weeks—a month actually. I sprained my ankle three weeks ago, and am pretty sure I have frostbite or something on my toes."

"Let's start with the toes. We'll see what we can do there then move onto your less serious concerns."

"Right." She unlaced the boots as far as possible before tugging them off. The toes of her socks looked wet again and she peeled them away. Nausea hit her stomach like a blow. The smell was acrid, a horrid combination of mildew, old shoe, and rot. "Fuck."

"I'll say." The doctor snapped his mask over his nose and crouched down. "This isn't good."

"Frostbite?"

"Yes." He pulled a cotton swab from a drawer and unwrapped it. "This might hurt, but I have to see how deep the damage is."

"Yeah." Nel knew she should look away, but her body didn't seem to want to listen to her brain. The three smallest toes on her left foot were entirely black. The skin was puffy and cracked as if someone had made up her feet to look like some monsters. The other toes were angry and swollen, but remained red, as were the toes on her right foot. The doctor prodded the skin around the blackened flesh. "It doesn't." Her voice shook, and it sounded very far away.

"Doesn't hurt?"

"No. Not those ones." She couldn't bring herself to clarify, but by his expression, he didn't need her to. "Am I going to lose them?"

He rested a hand on hers. "If I don't take them you could get incredibly sick and die."

"I know." And she did. The part of her brain that clearly had control of her mouth seemed unfazed. The rest of her balked, rampaging through a thousand stories she had heard about toes being essential for balance. The doctor rose and produced a plastic bucket from under the tiny sink in the corner. Nel stared at it, confused for a moment. Then her stomach caught up with her brain, then, and she vomited.

"I'll get you some things and show you to a bathroom. We'll have you clean up, and then we'll check your vitals and tend any other injuries. When was the last time you ate?"

"Yesterday. Had granola."

"I know you're hungry, but we ought to take care of things sooner. Assuming everything else checks out, I can fit you in this afternoon."

Nel nodded. His voice was a faint roar in her ears, thought she understood enough to answer his litany of questions about her past reactions to anesthesia and whether she would prefer a spinal. The hallway was deserted as the doctor escorted her to another small room. This one held a shower stall, towels, and another johnny.

"I'll send someone in a minute with the paperwork. Wash yourself and dress. You'll feel better. I promise."

She listened as the door locked behind him. She glanced in the corners of the room for cameras, then gave up and stripped. If they wanted a show, so be it. The shower seemed to have two settings: Arctic and Volcanic Spring. She settled for the latter and stepped inside. The provided soap was abrasive and smelled like a hospital, which, she realized after a moment, was fitting. It turned her abused body pink, but she scrubbed every inch she could reach. She refused to look at her feet, though she stubbed her dead toes more than once as she shambled about while she dried and dressed. Her johnny was an industrial teal that did nothing to put her at ease.

She wrapped a dry towel around her shoulders and perched on the bench. Every time she caught a glimpse of the blackened flesh, she fought the urge to puke. Guilt crouched in her gut. She frowned. What did she have to be guilty over? It was her own body. *But I could have prevented this somehow, I'm sure.* She scraped her hair back and checked her face in the mirror. *Fuck.* Her eyes were brown holes sunk in the battered tan of her skin. Skinny did not look good on her. She scrubbed the industrial lotion over her skin, wincing at the cold. In less than an hour she would lose a part of herself. Tiny parts, maybe, ones that she had never really appreciated, but parts of her body.

A sharp knock startled her and she swiped at her cheeks. "Come in."

The Suit stepped in. His coat was gone and he carried a manila envelope. "Hello again, Dr. Bently. You're more comfortable now, I trust?"

"It wasn't difficult." She tightened her grip on the towel. The juxtaposition between the starched suit and her own hospital-chic was not lost on her. *Time to turn the tables, in whatever way I can.* "You want to tell me why I'm here?"

The man frowned. "We've been looking for you for a month, Dr. Bently. You didn't make it easy."

"No fucking shit, you think I was going to turn myself in?"

The man frowned. "On the contrary, you asked. 'Wouldn't mind a ride' were your exact words, if I recall."

Nel swore she felt the floor lurch as her world toppled upside down. "What? Where am I?"

"We've been trying to get you here to safety since we got the news. This is the

Canadian Branch of the Institute for the Development of Humanity."

Relief flooded through her body, replaced a moment later by rage. She flung herself across the tiny room and jammed a starvation-sharpened elbow into the man's throat. "You fuckers!"

He pushed her away, face twisting with frustration. "Christ! Lin didn't lie about you. You're a nightmare."

The room spun and Nel found herself sitting on the floor. "I think I'm going to be sick."

"Not on me, you won't." He dropped the folder on the bench beside her and nudged the trashcan over with one polished shoe. "I can't believe you didn't know. Though it does explain some things." He shook his head. "Most of it, actually."

"Why didn't you just tell me who you were? All those times you almost caught me? You could have rolled down the window and waved me over."

"What times?"

Nel held up a hand, ticking the instances off on her fingers as she went. "First, when I was in Bethlehem buying this god-awful hair dye. Second, at Annie's house when you creeps stalked around the house like damned cops and I almost pissed myself. Third, when you actually caught me and treated me like a fucking psychopath."

The man sat back. "Christ, I told them we were on the right trail. We thought we caught glimpses of you, especially in Bethlehem, but you know how many disgusting hikers are in these woods? How many tips the cops got?"

"Were you working with them or something?"

"One of our men is dating the detective on the case. His boyfriend doesn't know he's telling us, though." The man shrugged.

"You didn't know? Why didn't you just track me with the GPS or something? Or say you'd pick me up at some location at some time?"

"The phone we gave you wasn't outfitted with GPS, we knew the cops would track it just as easily as we could. We were triangulating your position based on your texts and signal and tower locations. It was hell, honestly, but the cops could do it too, and we didn't know who else you were contacting. As for the last bit, we thought you could call a friend to drive you up to Oromoncto or something. It wasn't until a few weeks ago that we realized they were hunting you harder than we anticipated. We couldn't risk you being seen. By the time we realized we needed to get you ourselves, you were half starved and suspicious of everything. Rightly so, I guess."

"So you fucked up."

He eyed her. "There's no way I can get out of this without admitting it, eh?"

"Not really. No." As much as he was joking with her, she was tired, and about to let someone cut three of her toes off. She wasn't in the mood for banter. "So who are you?"

"I'm Captain Guillaume Sonier of the Canadian Army. Also, Executive Detective of the Institute for the Development of Humanity's Criminal Evaluation department."

"Criminal Evaluation?"

"Basically we work with people who are valuable to us and have committed a crime, or been framed for it, in your case. We make it possible to break them out or find ways to make their lives easier, hide them, or help them clear their names."

Relief spilled over Nel's head like hot water. "And you're going to clear my name?"

"Yes. As of tomorrow afternoon, if all goes according to plan, you'll be a free woman." He glanced down at her feet. "I'm told you have some papers to sign and a surgery to contend with?"

"Yes." She peered at the papers, making sure they were, in fact, consent to surgery, and signed on the various lines. She handed the clipboard back to him. "What now?"

"I'll deliver this to Dr. Bajwa and he'll get you sorted. We'll get you a room and food, clean clothes. You'll be stuck here until you've been cleared, but we'll do our best to make you comfortable."

Nel straightened. "Wait, my mom, I need to tell her I'm all right."

His eyes softened, but he shook his head. "Sorry, it'll have to wait until everything is made public. We can't have it seem like these events are orchestrated."

"Right." She sat back and watched him leave. This time the door didn't lock. Dr. Bajwa returned a moment later and showed her to the surgical bay. It was clean and stark, like everything in the base. She was greeted with pleasant indifference by the two nurses, and barely listened as they explained the preparation, the procedure, and her recovery. She nodded through it all.

A blue curtain over her waist blocked her from watching. The morbid part of her was curious, but the doctor shook his head when she asked if people ever watched.

"You don't need those images in your memory banks." She felt tugging, and faint pressure a few times, but otherwise, nothing. Her thoughts drifted, unable to stay on a single topic for too long. *Adavan is a miracle.* The only reoccurring thoughts were about where Lin might be and Mikey. An hour later she was blinking at the white ceiling and wondering how difficult it would be to walk again. Looking sidelong at her bandaged foot, she only had a sickening sense of "what have I done to myself?" She knew anger would come, and frustration at the Institute for her needless trek, but those stronger emotions had yet to claw through the haze of pain killers.

17

Nel scooted her wheel chair across the room as she hunted for the Ethernet password. The room was small and monochromatic, but outfitted with state-of-the-art technology, plush chairs and a queen-sized memory-foam bed.

"Doesn't do any good to make your cells out like a penthouse if I can't use any of it!" She slammed her hand on the desk. Despite knowing she wasn't arrested, the tiny room felt like prison. *Beside's I'm not allowed to actually leave, so is there much of a difference?*

Her foot was carefully wrapped in a plastic bag taped shut around her ankle. The massive fluffy bandage made looking at the offending limb easier. Loose sweatpants and a grey A-shirt completed her convict-or-dropout look.

A hesitant knock sounded at the door accompanied by the muffled sound of her name.

Nel thumbed the control to the door without thinking. *Maybe they'll know the internet password.* She glanced at the doorway. "What is it?" It took her a second to put the black hair, tattooed arm, and grace together. She launched herself from the chair and crossed the room with three hobbling steps. She pulled Lin down to her level with rough hands. "What the fuck, Lin?" She stopped any answer with two hard kisses.

Lin's eyes crinkled and she planted a third kiss on Nel's brow. "Maybe we can talk for a minute, get some things straightened out?"

"You've got some explaining to do."

Lin shrugged and tucked herself at the bottom of Nel's bed. "I missed you. Are you all right?"

"Well, I'm not dead, despite all evidence and efforts to the contrary." Nel hoisted herself back into the bed. As hard as her heart was pounding, she stayed just out of arm's reach. *I need conversation, explanations, not sex.* She dragged her eyes up from the neckline of Lin's white V-neck. *Well, explanations first at least.* "But I guess all right, yeah."

"Tell me everything?"

Nel narrowed her eyes. "Fine, but you got to give me two things first."

"What's that?"

"The internet password and some light brown hair dye."

Lin tapped a few lines of text into the watch at her wrist.

"That fancy alien tech? A 'wrist-com' or something?"

Lin's black brows arched. "It's a Google Watch, Nel. You forget that the Earth has surpassed most sci-fi predictions by now. Not our tech, yet, but there's plenty that makes life just as convenient and doesn't make us look like we're out of *Space Odyssey*."

Nel shrugged. "I'm bad with tech. Mikey made me get a smart phone—it did make organizing schedules as a teacher much easier, I'll give him that. But I think he mostly wanted me to play Pokémon." A sharp knock interrupted her trip down that rocky cul-de-sac off Memory Lane.

"The items you requested, Ms. Nalawangsa." The tone was distantly polite.

"Thank you." Nel leaned to the right, peering at the man at the door. She hadn't been aware that her cell came with room service.

The man was unremarkable and offered Nel a crisp nod. "Dr. Bently."

The door slid shut again. Lin held the hair dye aloft and tossed Nel a towel for her shoulders. "Victory."

Nel stripped her shirt off and climbed back into her chair with a half-hearted eye-roll. "You know what you're doing?" She jerked her chin at Lin's lengths of black hair. "Doesn't look like you've ever colored yours."

Lin frowned. "On the contrary. My natural hair color is bright green." At Nel's scowl, she winked. "Sorry. But I do know what I'm doing. My brother went through a rebellious phase where he changed his hair about every week." She dumped the contents of the box onto the bathroom counter and handed Nel the box. "That color all right?"

"Better than High-Vis-Orange."

"I don't know, with hair that color I won't lose you again."

Nel's hands stilled on the box. She refused to look up and meet Lin's eyes. *I'm not hers to fucking lose.* "I don't plan on getting lost again." She opened the dye jar before Lin could respond. "Let's get this done. And you can explain while you work, yeah?"

"Yeah." In the mirror, Lin's eyes were unreadable. Her face was smooth, expressionless.

Maybe I should cut her a little slack. This wasn't fun for anyone, really. Nel reached up and squeezed the other woman's hand. "Sorry, I'm just tired and in sore need of answers."

Lin flashed her a smile and scooped the dye onto Nel's head. Her gloved hands worked the color as close to the roots as she could. "I went back to the site the next day. After the fight. I phoned the Institute and explained what happened. After that I did what I could to protect the site."

"When I showed up there was caution tape and some cops, but they said it was just kids having a party in the desert. Let me take my equipment and cover up the units. That was it. I hated leaving those features open."

Lin's hands moved down to rest on Nel's toweled shoulders, leaving dark streaks where her fingers squeezed. "Those were Institute cops. I didn't tell them you were involved, so they spun you a lie."

Nel met her eyes in the mirror. "Why?"

"I wanted to protect you. I wanted you to get back home with your reputation, your life intact. That way when you published they couldn't argue, they wouldn't be prepared."

"My life intact? Lin, my entire world was turned on its head. My best friend is dead, my site destroyed and my permits revoked." She waved away Lin's apology. "Never mind. It's done. When did they find out?"

"When the body surfaced, they were going to let the cops arrest you. The fact that your DNA was there was perfect, a happy accident for them. I couldn't let that happened, though, so I told them everything. You knew too much, and besides, you're a damn good asset, so they decided to bring you in instead. Everything just seemed to go wrong, though." Lin shrugged. "The cops got wind that some of our people were connected and we spent weeks replacing our phones after we found a bug. It was a nightmare."

"You're telling me." Nel sighed.

"Your turn?"

"Yeah, just hand me my computer, I want to check my email." Nel started at the beginning, recounting her flight from UNE and the first weeks on the corridor. Her laptop balanced on her knee as she logged onto Chrome.

"And you were completely alone?"

"Well, I've two friends who were able to risk their futures by helping me. I found Annie—you never met her, but she was one of the students in Chile. She was my grad student.

She was running a CRM crew near Gorham and I accidently met up with them along the power lines. She saved my life, more than probably. From her place I canoed to where Tabby's staying."

"Tabby?"

"My ex."

Lin's brows rose and she seemed to want more of an explanation. Nel ignored her and opened her personal email. She winced at the volume of messages in her inbox. It would take months to sort through all of them. Her heart clenched as she saw half a dozen from her mother. That would be a long conversation, and one that would have to happen soon and probably in person. She glanced back up at Lin. "Anyways, after that it was hitchhiking and freezing my toes off—literally." She gestured to her foot. "You've got the quick version, and you'll get the long one later. Care to fill me in on the details of getting my name cleared? How clear are we talking? Will this show up on my record? What are they going to say actually happened?"

Lin fidgeted, one long leg bouncing as she eyes scanned the room. "Mind if I turn on the TV? There's something I need to show you."

She grabbed the remote off the bed and flicked the screen on.

Nel turned in her chair, gaze turning from Lin as she searched for some network to the flickering light of the television. It was some closed circuit channel, something she suspected was watched by evil men in a room full of screens. It showed a jostling view of the Antofagasta police department. Two officers pushed a cuffed man before them as they entered the building. At first the man refused to turn, but apparently one of the onlookers raised a good question.

He turned and Nel's brows arched. It was Emilio. His face was lined with fatigue and anger. Nel skimmed the closed captioning

EMILIO SEPULVEDA HAS BEEN ARRESTED FOR THE MURDER OF BASTIAN NUNÉZ, WHOSE BODY WAS FOUND TWO MONTHS AGO ON THE BEACH ALONG RTE 1. IN A STATEMENT SEPULVEDA RELEASED CONFESSING TO THE MURDER, HE SAID: "I HAD MY HERITAGE TO PROTECT. I DID WHAT I HAD TO DO. THE ARCHAEOLOGISTS WERE RUINING OUR LAND. I TOOK CARE OF THE MALE CREW CHIEF, AND WHEN

BAS ARGUED WITH MY DECISION, THE FIGHT ESCALATED. I DO NOT REGRET MY BELIEFS, BUT I DO REGRET HOW THINGS ENDED."

"What the hell is this, Lin?" Nel asked. "That doesn't sound like Emilio. At all. That sounds like garbage he's been fed. How did you frame him?"

"I explained the situation to him and he agreed to take the fall. We're taking care of him."

"Taking care of him? He'll be in prison for the rest of his life."

"Nonsense. He'll be transferred to another prison in exchange for giving up the names of others of Los Pobladores. While there he'll have a bad reaction to some standard inoculation and 'die.'" Lin's longer fingers crooked around the last word. "After that he's ours."

"So you've bought him off for information. He scratches your back if you scratch his? Doesn't explain why he confessed in the first place."

"Some details came to light—his involvement with the vandalism, the death of several of his friends and his inability to explain his whereabouts at the time of both Mikey's death and Bastian's."

"You blackmailed him. You sick fuck. Who really killed that man?"

"I did." Lin's eyes were steady, and for the first time in a long time Nel was abruptly reminded that Lin wasn't from Earth. *She might be human, but only as far as her genetics.* "We've cleared your name. You've got a unique way of saying 'thank you.'"

Contentment soured in Nel's stomach. "You think I should thank you? That I should be grateful?"

Lin's smile clattered from her face. "Well, we brought you here. And cleared your name."

"Are you kidding me? You think you did me a favor? Dude, I was suspected of murder. You think saying, 'Oh it was this chick I banged, but she can't come in for arrest since she's from outer fucking space,' would really work as an excuse?" Anger surged through her body. "I almost died of exposure alone on a damned power-line corridor. You realize how long it would have taken for people to find my body? I'd be nothing but coyote scraps. You show up, thinking I'm gonna thank you? I kinda wish I'd suggested you go fuck yourself instead of me."

Lin's brows crept steadily higher throughout Nel's rant. By the end her mouth twisted with dismay. "I'm so sorry, Nel. I know it means nothing, and it's too late, and I should have thought more about what this would do to you. You have to believe that I had no other choice. Emilio's taking care of it now."

"Framing someone else won't make me feel better about the situation."

"If you hear me out you might understand things a bit more." Her hand tightened on the doorknob and she stepped back. "It's impossible to talk to you when you're like this, though, so I'll discuss it when you're a bit more clearheaded."

"Clear-fucking-headed? Are you serious? When you pull that pretentious alien stick out of your ass, come talk to me." Nel wheeled across the room and jerked the door out of Lin's hand. *She's lucky I'm not a violent person.* "Get the fuck out." The door nearly hit Lin as it shut with a bang.

Fury exploded through Nel. Usually she ran, or walked it off. Her foot was an iron ball at the end of her body's chain. She hated being out of control. Her fist came down on the desk top, rattling the faux-wood surface. "Dammit!"

"She doesn't know any better."

"She's a piece of shit, is what," Nel snarled. "This is a joke. This entire organization is a joke. It's like I walked into bad fan fiction of the *X-Files,* and no one decided to inform me that I'm dating the alien." She stopped herself, realizing that there was a high possibility that she was being recorded, or, at the very least, Lin was still waiting in the hall, hearing Nel fall to pieces.

♠

Nel sat on the shower floor. Even the heat of the water wasn't enough to erase the sick feeling in her stomach. She spent weeks wishing more than anything that her name would be cleared. Now it was, but at the expense of a man's freedom. She wrapped her arms around her legs and pressed her knees into her eyes. Scalding tears followed the water's trail down her skin.

"Nel, you all right?" Lin's voice was low.

"Yes."

"You've been in there a while."

"I wasn't able to have a hot shower for weeks. Forgive me if I'm a little extravagant now," she sneered.

"I'm not worried about the planet." There was a pause, then she continued, her voice closer. "OK, obviously I am, but one woman's shower isn't going to make or break it right now."

"What do you want, then?" Nel watched the other woman's shadow moved across the room to the sink.

"I wanted to talk."

"I think you've said quite enough for the both of us."

"Yeah. Dar always said I talk too much and think too fast. It's gotten me into trouble a fair amount. It's kind of why I ended up on earth."

"I thought you were doing your dissertation here."

"It's a long story. What I'm saying, though, is that I messed up. I know it. I wasn't the one who came up with the idea to frame Emilio, but I sure didn't stop them. We have so much power, Nel, sometimes it's hard to realize that most people don't. I've been taught to think of what we do as good, for the better. I never realized there are other ways to look at it. Worse ways."

"No kidding." Nel leaned back against the tub, enjoying the sting of high water pressure. "Next time, maybe lead with the 'we're going to spring him out' part of the plan, rather than the 'we blackmailed a guy into confessing to murder.'"

"I guess I didn't realize how close you and he were."

"We're not, Lin." Nel sighed. "There's another side effect to growing up in space—you guys have a place to go, other humans to rely on, scattered across the stars. Here on Earth, all we've got is each other. It's just us piloting this rock through a vacuum."

"I'm sorry." Lin's level voice was soft. "Really, I am. I'll make this right. I promise. I don't want to lose you."

Nel snorted, even though the other woman's words caused something in her chest to jump. "You barely know me."

Something shifted outside the curtain then Lin slipped into the shower, naked. Her eyes were red, but weeping looked far better on her than most women. She sat on the floor of the tub too, her long legs folding around Nel's. "I realize that. I don't know your favorite song, or food. I don't know where you grew up, or what your favorite thing to do as a child was. I don't know what your parents do for a living. I don't know what you wanted to be when you grew up." She reached out, running tentative fingers down Nel's cheek. "I don't know you at all, but I really want to."

Her hands were warm satin against Nel's skin. Her palms slid up Nel's legs, tickling the fine blonde hairs. Her gaze followed, as if examining something she had never seen before. Her thumb paused on a hooked scar on Nel's knee.

"I fell a long time ago. Slipped on chicken shit in my friend's driveway." Nel offered the story, her voice seeming too loud in the tiled room. Her hands found Lin's shoulders. They were too tired to do much more than draw circles against the beige skin under her fingers.

Lin lowered her head to Nel's legs, dropping chaste kisses in the wake of her hands. She moved higher, her fingers sure and gentle all at once. The shower water pattered over her damp hair, sending rivulets down her brow and nose to glide onto Nel's skin with each kiss.

"I don't think I can—"

"I wasn't going to." Lin's touch was tender, rather than sexual. Instead of a massage that dragged tension from her body and left Nel aching, Lin's fingers erased sorrow and anger.

"You've been alone for a long time. Not just with running and Mikey. Before that, I think."

Nel nodded and leaned her head back. The water was a tickling counterpart to Lin's attention, and she let her eyes lid. The silence was punctuated by Nel's murmurs of pleasure and Lin's low laugh. The water grew tepid, and despite Lin's warm hands, goose bumps erupted up Nel's arms.

"One second." Lin slipped from the shower, leaving a chill in her absence. Nel toed the shower off. She eased herself up and shoved the curtain aside. Lin held a thick, white towel. Nel stepped into the outstretched towel, letting Lin wrap it around her shoulders and envelope her in the warmth of her arms for a moment.

Nel glanced up at their reflection in the mirror. "I don't even recognize myself, Lin."

"You've had a hard few weeks." Lin took the corner of her own towel and dried Nel's face.

"That's not how I meant."

"I recognize you."

"You never knew me. You didn't know the Nel that Mikey knew. I was so sure, of everything. If I faced a choice, I'd choose.

There was no angst, no confusion. I knew what I wanted, even when I was little."

"You don't feel like that now?"

"No. I've been lost. And it's not just because of Mikey, though that's part of it, I know. It's something else. I knew where I was going, where I wanted to be. And now?" She shrugged. "I don't think I want it anymore, but I can't figure out why the hell I changed my mind."

"You're still determined and certain, Nel. You just aren't choosing things that you expected." She tucked a newly blonde lock of Nel's hair behind her ear. "What can I do to help you? To show you that you've not lost yourself?"

Nel glanced up. "Honestly?"

"Yeah?" Lin leaned forward, fingers lacing with Nel's. "Anything."

Nel looked up. She watched the excitement fade form Lin's eyes at whatever expression crossed her own. "I want to go home. Now. I don't want to wait for some legal shit to clear. Captain Sonier says I'm free, so I'm free."

"I can drive you."

"Fine, but I need to be alone. Drive there, sing '99 Bottles of Beer on the Wall' the whole way down, if you want. Just let me be home alone."

Lin looked down, but nodded. "I get it."

Nel withdrew her hand. "You really don't, but thanks for trying."

18

"I'll call you, all right?"

"Yeah." Nel stared at her front door. Part of her had wondered if she would ever see it again.

"Nel, did you hear me?"

"Yeah, I did." She finally glanced at Lin with a faint smile. "You'll call. And I'll answer." She tugged her bag from the seat. "Talk to you soon." After a swift peck on the mouth, Nel sidled out of the car. She waited at the end of her walk while the driver pulled away. The street was deserted. The sky was almost dark, the cold of winter biting on the wind. She drew a breath, then another, before retrieving the spare key from the mouth of the frog statue by the door.

She'd have to get her car at the impound lot, but that was a problem for future Nel to deal with. Present Nel was only interested in bed and a beer. The door swung open, unlocked. The kitchen light was on, and a fire in the hearth lit the living room. She stopped, the forgotten door banging against the wall. She could hear someone moving down the hall. "Mikey?" The plea was a whisper, almost a prayer, almost a curse.

"Honey, is that you?" Her mom emerged from the kitchen.

Nel got as far as an exhausted smile before she was wrapped in a hard, warm hug. "Hey, Mom."

"Christ, I was so worried for you. I didn't know what to think, except they were wrong, they had to be wrong." She pulled back, scanning her daughter for injury. "You're all right? You're safe? They realized it was all a mistake? I was so worried."

"Something like that. I've had a long month." She deposited her bag by the door. "I don't suppose you left me any beer?"

Her mom wrinkled her nose. "I'm not a fan of your fancy foreign stuff."

"It's not foreign, Mom, it's a microbrew. About as American as you get." Nel moved into the kitchen, going through the subconscious motions of grabbing a beer and popping off the top. "You lit a fire?"

"Yeah." Her mom looked away, sweeping a lock of her shoulder-length, grey-brown hair from her tired eyes. "Made the place feel a bit more homey."

"It's nice." Nel followed her into the living room and flopped onto the couch. "I suppose this is the part where I get grilled?"

Her mom's brows curled. "Well, I'd like to know where you've been. What really happened. You're always so certain, love. You never waver, never question yourself. When you came back from Chile, after Mikey...all you did was question things." She sat at the other end of the couch, her legs tucked under herself. It reminded Nel of Lin, and she looked away.

"I'm sorry, Mom."

"Sorry? Baby, I'm just worried for you."

"There was some stuff about the site, that was political. And we pissed off the wrong people. I made it out, but Mikey didn't. After he died, my backers sent in the big guns. There was a fight, and I don't remember half of it. Someone must have died. Because I was there, and a foreigner, they thought it was me."

"That's ridiculous."

"Not really. It could have been. When I was at my lowest, I thought it might have been." She looked down.

"I don't believe that you could have killed someone."

"Mom, I love you, but everyone can kill someone. It's just how easily they can do it that matters." She looked down. "Anyways, my backers knew it wasn't me, so they gave me the address of a safe place. It took me two months to get there, but I did it. I was able to meet the bigwigs. And then Lin told me Emilio confessed." She stared at the fire. She hated that she was corroborating the false story, that she was blaming Emilio for Bastian's murder. But she couldn't tell anyone the truth. Not even her mother.

"Lin?"

"The woman who came to help out in Chile."

"Ahh. Of course."

"What?" Her eyes narrowed. "What's 'of course'?"

"There's always a woman, isn't there." Her mother's smile was broad and knowing.

"Don't look at me like that." Nel took a deep sip of her beer and glared at the label. "I didn't say she was special."

"No, but you suddenly don't know which way is up. Part of that is grieving. Part of it is falling."

"I don't love her."

Her mom took her hand. "No, of course not. You don't know her hardly enough for my tastes. But you'd like to. And that's how it starts." Her brown eyes warmed. "That's how it was with your father."

"Great." Nel rolled her eyes. "You guys fought all the time."

"That wasn't because we didn't love each other." Her face was both bright and sad. "I trust that you'll make the right choice. You always do, even if I don't realize it at the time."

Nel scooted closer and leaned over, head resting on her mom's shoulder. "I'm really glad you were here."

"Well, your plants won't water themselves, Honey."

Nel hummed in response. She was warm, and home, and just for a second she had no choices to make. "Are you going home tonight?"

"I hadn't planned to. I've been staying in the spare room. Your bed's made, though, with clean sheets." She glanced toward the kitchen, where the phone rested. "I should call Bill, let him know you're back."

"You should. Wouldn't want him to worry." She pushed herself up with a groan. "I'm going to take a shower."

"Want me to order some take-out? Maybe from that falafel joint? It should get here by the time you're out."

Nel turned from her hunt for a towel and wrapped her mom in another hug. "I love you. You're the best mom."

"I'll get you the spicy falafel pocket, then."

Nel squeezed her tighter for a moment then stepped away with a watery smile. "And cabbage and lentil salad please. I'm fucking starving." She ducked into the bathroom. The fact that her mom let the cursing slide told her exactly how worried she had been. She showered quickly, more for practicality than relaxation, and donned her favorite pajamas before returning to the living room.

Mindi had set up the coffee table and was busy unpacking the just-delivered takeout. She glanced up, eyes widening at Nel's clothing. "Good God, Anna, what is that?"

"Adult onesie. Mikey and I had matching ones."

"I will never again wonder why either of you were single. That thing is horrendous. And why does it say 'Excrement' all over it?"

"It's 'Exterminate,' Mom, and it's a Doctor Who reference. Mikey's was all about the Doctor. Mine is one of his enemies. Never got into the sci-fi stuff myself, but he loved it. Ironic, really."

"How's that?"

Nel looked down. *Because I'm diddling an alien chick and my site was the scene of a 13,000 year old UFO sighting.* "Just 'cause everything seems to be so weird all of a sudden. Feels like the *X-Files* half the time, with all the weird government stuff."

"But it's over, right?" Mindi piled food onto her plate, glancing at Nel out of the corner of her large brown eyes.

"I guess, yeah." Nel tucked into her salad, not caring that she probably had oil and tahini all over her face. "I don't know what I'll do about school. I doubt I'll be able to go back. Everything is kind of up in the air right now."

Mindi paused, her lamb wrap poised half way from her plate. "Honey, you know you're always welcome at home."

"I don't think Bill would love a thirty-something lesbian kipping on his couch."

"We have a guest room, Anna, and he's gotten over whatever it was that had him so upset."

You mean when he walked in on me sleeping with his friend's daughter? "Yeah, maybe. I've got to hash out some stuff before I go making life changes." She wrapped up the second half of her meal. Weeks of starvation made her stomach too small to handle much more than a big snack. She curled up at the end of the couch and watched her mom polish off her meal. "What was Dad like? I mean, when he was young? I know the stories about his childhood, and you two before you had me. But what about the rest of it?"

Mindi sat back, staring at the fire thoughtfully. One hand rested on Nel's foot, rubbing tiny circles and pinched her toes like she had when her daughter was little. "He was always a mysterious man. Even when I thought I knew everything about him, it was like there were depths I'd never know. He was so strong, so certain of everything in his world. It was like loving a sequoia—this impossible thing that withstood time and storms and progress." Her laugh was soft. "But impossible nonetheless. I wish you had gotten to know him the way I did—things change when you start to see your parents as humans, not just caregivers."

"Me too." Nel's eyes roved to her mantelpiece. Two wooden boxes flanked the pop-surrealist artwork hanging above the fireplace. The left held some of Mikey's ashes, the right, her father's. She could feel her eyes lidding as she listened to her mother's voice. The warmth of the fire and Mindi's words cocooned her with comfort, and she couldn't bring herself to go to bed.

19

Nel woke up, groggy, her neck twisted at an odd angle. She was still on the couch. The sounds of running water and the smell of coffee were evidence that her mom was already up. She tossed aside the blanket Mindi must have laid over her and stretched. A grunt served as greeting to her mother on her way into the bathroom. She flicked on her phone as she sat on the toilet. Monday. 9:42.

She groaned. She would have to face the horrible, dissonant music that was the anthropology department. She washed her hands and face, raking her hair back before peering in the mirror. She looked a damn sight better than she had a week ago. The hollows under her eyes and in her cheeks were almost filled in. "What do you think? Think I can get my job back?"

"They'll be wary about parents' concerns, but there's no ground for them to stand on to actually fire you."

"But what if I don't want to go back."

"This is what you've always wanted."

"No, this is what I thought I was supposed to want."

Mindi's soft knock interrupted the imagined conversation. "Honey, you all right? You talking to someone on the phone?"

"Just talking to myself, Mom." She pulled open the door. "I'm not looking forward to meeting with the school board." She took a sip of the mug her mom pressed into her hand. "Kind of wish I could just be a kid for a day, you know?"

"Well, if you wear those pajamas to your meeting they'll give you a nice room with soft walls and a snuggling jacket that hugs you." She smiled. "What time is your meeting?"

"Eleven, but I wanted to talk to Martos. Get a bead on the situation, you know? What were your plans today?"

"If you don't need anything else I was going to head back down to Peekskill. I've been away a while and God only knows what Bill's been feeding himself."

"Would it kill the man to learn to cook? Even, like, lasagna?"

"Just because you reject traditional gender roles, my dear, does not mean everyone does.

Besides, I've seen the bathroom—I can imagine what my kitchen would look like after he was done with it." She whacked Nel lightly on the behind with her gossip magazine. "Get ready, I'll drop you off on my way out of town, all right?"

Nel snorted and traipsed into her room. Professional clothes felt strange after her time in hiding. It took her a minute's searching before she realized her favorite dress boots were forgotten somewhere on a power line corridor. She scraped her hair into some semblance of order, glaring the entire time at the stranger in the mirror. She missed her hair, but she had to admit even a pixie-cut was an improvement from Incarceration Orange. "Mom, you have any makeup?"

Mindi peered into her daughter's room. "You're serious?"

"Well, I look like death and would rather present a collected and alive persona than 'I'm gonna eat yer brainzzz.'" She stared at the bag her mother tossed her, eyes narrowed. "I might need some help."

"I've finally got a real girl for a child." At Nel's injured expression, she rolled her eyes. "I'd never want any kid but you, sour-puss." She dabbed pink powder onto Nel's cheeks and temples, peered at her handiwork, then added another spot to the bridge of her nose. "There. Thank goodness we have the same coloring, eh?"

✦

The conference room was warm, and a fat fly tapped a lazy dance across the window. Out of anxiety, Nel arrived early, but sitting alone, waiting for the board to arrive made her nerves decidedly worse. She had half a dozen prepared speeches, but had no idea what to actually expect. *Not to mention, what they've been told.* She knew vague details of what the Institute had claimed to get her name cleared, but between the pain killers for her toes and the general confusion of her life, the details had fallen through the cracks in her mind.

She arranged the stack of papers from her bag again. *Copy of my contract, writ proclaiming my innocence.* She wondered which they'd spend the most time on. The door swung open and Martos peered in.

"God, Bently." He wheeled over as she scrambled from her seat to hug him. "I had to get here early to see you," he mumbled into her shoulder. "I almost didn't believe them when I got the email that you were back, and all right." His arms tightened before he released her. He searched her face. "Are you all right? You're wearing make-up."

She snorted. "I'm OK. Been better, but I'm OK." She sank back into her chair and gestured at her foot. "Had a bit of an accident, but still have seven of my toes."

"Only seven?" He shook his head. "Don't tell me, my muesli and yogurt might make a reappearance." He squeezed her hand and jerked his head at the semi-circular table. "I'd best get settled."

Nel remained silent as the other four board members filed in over the next few minutes, offering them only a nod in greeting. If she opened her mouth now, she was sure vomit would accompany whatever words squeaked past her heart lodged in her throat.

Finally, Dr. Heng cleared her throat and leaned forward. "Dr. Bently." She slid her glasses down to fix Nel with her dark eyes. "Thank you for joining us."

"Thank you for having me. This meeting is overdue."

Heng's brow twitched, as if she was trying to determine whether Nel meant anything sarcastic by the words. "Indeed. Let's get the messy business out of the way first, shall we?"

She scanned whatever document before her through her readers. "I have a letter here from the Institute for the Development of Humanity. They corroborate what the FBI said. That you were falsely accused of murder and were put into protective custody for the past few months."

First I've heard of it. "Correct. I had information on the actual murderer, but I feared for my safety. The departments apparently weren't the best at communication and it took a bit for the entire mess to be sorted. But here I am now."

"And you've also applied for tenure?"

Martos shot a glance at Nel, clearly willing her to play along. "Also, long overdue."

She gave him a wan smile. *Of course it was you who applied in my name.* "I was encouraged to do so before this semester. Obviously some things got in the way." *Biggest understatement of the entire Holocene.*

"Well," Heng leaned forward, "there are obviously some pretty large issues with granting you tenure. You were accused of murder. Cleared, yes, but with the number of reactive, overprotective parents that pay tuition to this institution, you can see our concern."

Martos cleared his throat. "I doubt very much that the anthropology department makes up enough of that tuition to even make a dent."

Heng shot him a look, but her full lips curled. "Be that as it may, we must treat this with the same weight as if it were the Biology Department. Your four years here as an Adjunct have been unremarkable—both a pro and a con. Your students are driven and have done well in their chosen fields, but your reviews are often fraught with some colorful feedback." She pulled out a handful of photocopied review notes. "'*Dr. Bently rarely sees the good in a student, or the potential, focusing only on areas to improve and offering constructive, but negative, feedback.*' Another claims '*Dr. Bently and her standards are the reason I quit Anthropology.*'"

Nel winced and looked down. "Positive feedback is something I'm working on."

"I think you misunderstand my purpose in reading these. Your personal life, specifically in the past few months, might be colorful, and leave much to be desired in the way of stability. However, this feedback comes from Freshmen and Sophomore level students. You drive them hard. You take your position here extremely seriously, and lend the

Anthropology department a hard edge that it might otherwise lack. You are the 'bad cop' to the late Dr. Servias' 'good cop,' so to speak."

Nel sat back. Her heart hammered in her chest. It didn't sound like a refusal. It sounded like the opposite. *So why do I feel overwhelmed? Why do I feel like running?* "Who's the good cop now?"

Martos shrugged. "There's plenty of professors here who have gained the department a reputation for being an easy one. We could stand to change that."

"What are you saying?"

"We discussed this yesterday, in preparation for this meeting. You've been absent for this semester, and there will be a lot to iron out in the next few months, but we're prepared to grant you tenure starting next fall." Heng rose and slid the document across the table to Nel.

Martos caught her eye. "If you're still interested, that is."

Her mind kept tripping over the future, over all she had learned about the world, about herself in the last months. *"Think of how far we've come. We'll make it."* But if Lin's brother was right, humanity wouldn't make it, not unless every person started shouting. Not unless every person rose up, fist in the air. Nel looked down at the contract, at the pile of dense words she used to dream about. A tinny chirp interrupted her meditation and she glanced down at her pack. There were only two people who used that number. She flipped open the phone. Two messages.

TO: DR. ANNALISE BENTLY
OFFER OF EMPLOYMENT:
HEAD OF IHD DEPT OF CULTURAL EXPLORATION
TIME SENSITIVE: RESPOND BY 10/04

Nel winced. Head of an international anthropology department? *Two dreams come true, warring with each other.* Too good to be true, and there was a catch for both, she was certain.

"Dr. Bently, do you have something more pressing?"

Her heart was pounding again, but for an entirely different reason. "You asked me to take a moment to think it over. That includes all my options."

"You have another standing offer?"

"So it would appear. One moment, please." She softened the words with a flashed smile and opened the second message, this one heralded by the grainy contact picture of Lin, hair blown loose and sun rising behind her.

IDH JUST TEXTED YOU, I THINK.
I'D LOVE TO WORK WITH YOU.
WE CAN'T DO THIS ALONE.
PLEASE?

Uncertainty twisted with resentment. She was tired of being a tool. She was tired of letting Lin rule her life. *So accept the role of bishop to her pawn, and play the game.* Besides, as frustrating and idealistic as the woman was, she was strong and clever, and Nel had never been able to pass up that combination. She dropped the phone into her pocket and straightened. Calluses scratched at the sheaf of papers she had hoped to see for the last ten years. "Thank you so much for your consideration. I'm honored at your support, and I've grown so much from my time here at UNE."

"This sounds like a resignation."

She looked up at Dr. Heng. "It is. I've been offered the position at Institute for the Development of Humanity as the head of their anthropology department."

"And you plan to accept it?" The soft, rumbled voice was Martos. His eyes were misted, his smile sad.

Nel swallowed hard. "I do. Again, thank you for your consideration." A smile bloomed on her face, lit with an impish light she learned from Lin. "Maybe next time." She gathered her things and stepped from the room. She slipped her phone out as soon as the door clicked shut behind her.

RE: OFFER OF EMPLOYMENT...
ACCEPTED.

20

The box on her desk was bursting. Nel had no idea how she accumulated so much in her four years as a professor at UNE. Martos's knock was soft on her half-open door. She glanced up from wrestling another book into a corner of the box. "Hey."

"Hey." He fiddled with the worn arm of his chair. "You're wasting no time."

She turned back to the mess of papers from classes she hadn't taught in two years. "I'm not sure when I'm supposed to start."

"You're sure this isn't too fast? You're still grieving, and familiar places seem so empty when you're missing someone. You shouldn't run from that loneliness, you know. It's tough, but you have to sit with it a while. It took me years before I could stand myself after Judy died."

She forced her hands to still. "Mikey wasn't my partner."

"Platonically, maybe. Those lines are blurred when you work together as long as you two did." His eyes were unreadable when they met hers. "I'm worried you're making a mistake."

"Do you remember the first time you told me to forget tenure?" she asked.

"Yes. I said you were too angry and fast-paced. And I distinctly remember you shouting that I was a misogynist and you had a right to feel before slamming my door."

"Right. That." She heaved a sigh. "You said I was too angry. Mikey said the same. And you're right, both of you were right. It fueled that determination, that hard edge Dr. Heng mentioned. But this anger is the only thing inside me now, the only thing left. As long as I run at 98 percent I'll never slow down enough for everything to catch up, yeah? So instead of choking myself to fit into a job I thought I wanted, I'm channeling it into a job that needs me."

"I think that's the most you've ever said without swearing."

"Fuck off."

"There we go." His dark hands laced and he looked away. "What is it, this job?" He raised a finger. "Not just what they said, what actually is it? Where will you go?"

Nel stopped. She had no idea. She never thought to ask. "Um, some of the details are still up in the air."

"Nel, you know nothing about these people."

"I know enough about one of them. Enough to trust her." It was a lie, a small one, but it was the only thing she had. Her phone chirruped, and she flicked it open.

"It's them, isn't it? They're the reason you disappeared for two months."

"No, I disappeared for two months because I was framed for murder and on the run from the law."

"Framed? I thought you were in protective custody."

"Right. Yeah. But framed by...it's complicated." Her gaze fell to the new message.

BE READY AT 4PM. I'LL COLLECT YOU OUTSIDE YOUR HOUSE.

She rolled her eyes and thumbed a quick response, asking if she should pack.

LIGHTLY, BUT BRING ANYTHING REALLY IMPORTANT. CARRY-ON BAG ONLY.

"I'll give you this, Martos, they are secretive bastards." She glanced at the clock above her desk and blanched. 3:27 PM. "Fuck, I've got to go."

"Already?"

"Yeah, Lin just texted. She's picking me up at 4:00 and I gotta pack." Nel hoisted the box onto her hip. "I'll get the rest of this sorted later." Martos's frown made her pause. "What is it?"

"I feel as if this is good bye." He beckoned her down. "I'll miss you. Profanities and temper and all."

She squeezed him tightly. "I'll miss you too. And I'll email. Promise." His dry hand was feather-light on the back of her neck as he planted a kiss on her brow before letting her straighten. They were silent as he wheeled down the hall beside her. When she turned back at the department door he just raised a hand. "Stay safe, Dr. Bently."

♠

Back at home she dragged out her various carry-on bags. For someone who traveled a lot, she had far too much luggage. *Bring anything really important.* After two months without any supplies, she knew what was important. *They'll provide practical things. I should only grab sentimental, personal stuff.* Sentimental implied unnecessary. Still, her hands stopped on Mikey's leather field pack. He was always better prepared than she.

"Take it. It's got the most room and you know it."

"I just keep expecting you to need it back." She tucked her personal tools into the front pouch with her wallet and passport. She grabbed her two favorite books and the tiny panda bear that came from the hospital gift shop when she was born. *Fuck. Mom.* She shoved a few changes of clothes after her toothbrush and laptop case.

She dialed twice before allowing the call to ring through. "Hey, Bill, it's Nel. My mom there?"

She listened to her stepdad pressing the phone into his chest to shout, "Mindi, it's Anna!" After a second he returned. "She'll get you upstairs."

"Thanks."

The phone clicked once, then a warm voice crackled over the line. "Hey, sweetie. Everything all right? How'd the meeting go?"

"Hey, Mom. Yeah, everything's fine." She swallowed. "I, um, I actually got a new job."

"What? Those assholes fired you?"

Nel grinned. She never questioned where her own attitude came from. "No, the school actually offered me tenure."

The pause was long, and Nel could picture her mother shutting her study door and sinking into her favorite reading chair. "But you didn't take it?"

"No." Nel glanced out the window, watching a blue sedan slow to a stop in front of her driveway. "I actually don't have a lot of time, I've got a flight to catch. But the company that funded the Chile dig offered me a job. It's a pretty big deal. I'll be head of my own department and everything."

"Oh honey. I'm so proud of you. Your dad would be, too." Silence fell at the words and Nel listened to her mom swallow hard. There was something else in the tone, something that had laced Martos's voice, too.

"Yeah. I know." Nel watched Lin sprint up to the door, but ignored the first knock. "I think it'll take me a while to settle in, though, so I might be a bit radio silent."

"Where are you going?"

Nel shrugged, though she knew her mother couldn't see. "I don't really know yet, I've got to be briefed." She knew she never spoke like this, and it would only make her mother more suspicious, but she couldn't lie. "We won't have a ton of signal, I'm told, so communication is going to be slow and probably over e-mail, but as soon as I figure it out I'll give you updates."

"Let me know if you need me to check in on the house."

"I will, I love you."

"I love you, too, honey. Please keep in touch as much as you can. I'll miss you. Stay safe."

A shiver ran down Nel's spine as the words echoed Martos's. "Always."

"Don't disappear on me again, OK? I'll be forced to come after you this time, if you do. And let me know as soon as you're settled. Are you sure you're OK?"

"Yeah, just in a bit of a whirlwind, is all. I still need to figure a few things out. My ride's here now, and I've got to finish packing." She shoved her Zune and chargers into the pack, grabbing things at random as she scanned the room.

"OK. I love you, honey."

"I love you, too, Mom." She hung the phone up and went to the door. She pressed her forehead against the cool wood for a moment before tugging it open. "Hey, Lin."

"You ready? We're going to be late."

"I think so. Not really sure what to bring. Had to call my mom."

Lin paused, her brows curling together for a moment. "Your mom?"

"Yeah, why?"

"I guess I never thought of you having a family." She shook her head. "Never mind. Everything sorted?"

"I guess it has to be." Nel did a last round of her house, locking windows, locking doors, turning down the heat and flicking out lights. It seemed like both just a day and an eternity since she last went through her house, checking on everything after returning from Chile.

The sedan idled outside, the tinted windows preventing her from seeing whether there was a driver or if Lin had come alone. Nel tossed her bag into the trunk and slid into the rear seat. There was, indeed, a driver, and

Lin took the front seat. Nel had just buckled when she scrabbled at the door. "Wait!" She tumbled from the car, coming back to grab her keys from the cup holder, before ducking back into her living room. The two boxes of ashes sat on the mantle. She tucked them into her coat pocket before dashing back to the car. "All right, sorry. I'm good."

Lin glanced back with curiosity. "Forget something?"

"Yeah." Nel flashed her a smile. She wasn't ready to open up that part of her heart, but the kindness in Lin's eyes almost made her want to. Her fingers closed around the boxes in her pocket, still warm from last night's fire. *I'm not leaving you guys behind this time.*

21

Nel and Lin arrived at an abandoned warehouse after a two hour drive, a puddle-jumper flight amid stormy skies from Keene to Orormoncto, then another three hour drive north. Even with the care taken to allow the paint to chip and the windows to crack, Nel knew better. No abandoned warehouse had gleaming electric locks on the gate or multi-million dollar security systems hidden along the rooftop and in the trees. Lin slid aside a wooden shingle and typed in some long code.

The door clicked, then opened with a whir. Lin glanced back at Nel, as if to confirm she still stood a step behind her, then slipped inside. The interior of the building was as modern as the outside was unremarkable. Gleaming glass and steel replaced basic cinder blocks and rebar. Nel followed Lin, brows rising. "So we're meeting people now to hammer out the details before we go?"

"Not exactly, no." Lin looked down. "We're leaving for headquarters from here, actually."

Nel stopped in the middle of the gleaming corridor. She realized there were a dozen things she should have asked before leaving home. Once again, Lin had asked her to jump and her only question had been how high. "I thought this was just a quick meeting, not the actual job. How long will we be gone? I haven't finished cleaning out my office. I've got a car to return to Enterprise, a mortgage to pay." She threw her hands up. "I know I should have asked before, but seriously, Lin, this is sudden, even for you. And I don't even know where we're going. Like, at all."

Lin frowned. "You accepted the position, I assumed they gave you all the details."

Nel flashed the text at her. "That's all they gave me."

Lin's smile quirked her lips. "That's why I like you. You knew nothing—your salary, the location, the job description. Nothing. And you agreed" She hadn't stopped walking and Nel's tired legs ached as she jogged to keep up with the taller woman's long, graceful strides.

"You like me 'cause I'm a raging idiot?"

Lin stopped at the end of the hall and jabbed an elevator button. "Because you go with your gut."

"Try a bit lower."

Lin scoffed. "You can get laid without the fancy job." Her arms crossed, graceful even while stubborn. "So, are you going to renege?"

"I wasn't certain I could. Can you at least tell me where I'm going that I can't postpone until I've got things sorted here? And I don't even have a place to rent wherever I'll be working." Nel threw her hands in the air. She was tired of being without control. She was tired.

"I'm sure whatever financial ties you have will be taken care of. We're going to headquarters for your briefing. You'll be staying in Cabin 5491, and everything is time sensitive because our departure is weather-dependent."

"I don't suppose Headquarters is in Prague or Vienna or someplace I've always wanted to visit."

"Maybe when you were really little and still knew how to dream." The flashing lights lit Lin's face as the elevator plummeted into the facility. "You've got just under an hour to opt out."

"And if I do, what then?"

"You crawl back to UNE and beg forgiveness?"

"And what about bringing life-saving tech to Earth? Saving us from ourselves? All the things you told me about in Chile?" She could feel tension rolling from Lin with the other woman's effort to remain neutral.

"We'll manage like we always have— without you."

"And you? Would I see you again? Hear from you?"

"I'd email when I could, but there's not much signal where we're going."

Before Nel could ask, the elevator whirred open. Stark, white light seared her eyes and she blinked at the cavernous room beyond. The sunken middle of the hanger was cleared, save for the massive ship aimed at the ceiling. The engines already growled, steam and hydraulics hissing in the cold air. Like Lin, it was just to the left of normal. The sleek build was nothing she had ever seen in public aeronautical programs. The ceiling was shuttered, but Nel noted massive arms that would pull it apart when it came time for lift off. *Lift off.* Her mind stumbled over the idea.

A woman appeared beside them in a crisp lab coat. A slim metal clipboard perched in the crook of her arm. She ticked off two names as she nodded a greeting. "Dr. Bently, Ms. Nalawangsa. I'm Dr. Gull. Dr. Sukarno will brief you on departure protocol just over there."

"Actually, Dr. Bently's having second thoughts."

Dr. Gull waited as the overhead speaker barked, "T-45 MINUTES. ETD 01:00."

Nel did not hear whatever the woman explained next. Her eyes were fixed on the shuttle. *Departure. No signal. Weather dependent.* The pieces thudded into place like tumblers on the padlock around Nel's heart. Headquarters was a space station. "I'll do it."

"Excuse me?" Dr. Gull looked up from the note she had just made on her tablet.

"I'll go. Into space, to Headquarters, wherever. I'll go." She might have just accepted the booty-call of a century, but dammit, how many chances would she have at interstellar travel?

Lin ducked her head, but failed to hide her impish grin. "I'll show her to Check-In." Her hand was soft and firm in Nel's. "You'll have a chance to get your bearings once we're cleared."

"I don't think I'll ever get my bearings." Rage quieted its chattering in her mind, the cloud of grief and worry stilled its writhing. *I think that's why I'm doing this.*

♠

The glass-walled offices and conference rooms of the upper floor were a tech school's dream. Twice Lin had to drag Nel from peering at the de-briefings and mission control meetings in the dozen rooms on their way down the hall. She held the door at the end of the corridor open for Nel. Instead of a cavernous conference room, Nel stepped into a narrow, brightly lit office.

A dark man with a shaved head sat behind the array of computers sprawled across the desk. He wore what appeared to be a tightly fitted black jogging suit. He flashed them a smile, fingers skimming the glowing touch keyboard. Like everything Nel had encountered, it was just slightly too advanced for normal Earth technology.

"Isn't it a bit late to be finalizing trajectories, Captain?"

The man shook his head at Lin with a faint laugh. "You know Propulsion finalized the trajectory a month ago." He stood long enough to offer Nel his hand. "Dr. Bently, I presume?"

"Yes, Captain."

"I'm Dr. Dani Sukarno, Captain of the shuttle *Iman*. It's lovely to finally meet the woman who gave the Institute such a rough time of it. They may have paid my way through school, but I do love a good underdog."

There was only one other chair, and Lin seemed content to lean on the bookcase by the door. Nel sat. She kept her bag firmly between her boots. "So I'm here for briefing? Mind telling me a bit more about things? I think I've been incredibly sporting so far."

Sukarno sat back, steepling his fingers and bringing the full weight of his bright brown eyes to bear on her. "Of course. We don't have all the time in the world, but your curiosity is valid. Your real briefing will occur at Headquarters, but I'll bring you up to speed as much as I can now." He typed a few commands into his computer and turned one of the flat screen monitors around to face her.

Nel noticed, belatedly, that all the screens were floating. Despite the tech, the presentation that bloomed on the screen was your standard PowerPoint. It showed a blue planet that, aside from the expansive desert spread across one hemisphere, could have been Earth.

"Ms. Nalawangsa explained to you our particular relationship with Earth's inhabitants, correct?"

"A bit. I was grief-stricken and exhausted and sitting in a jeep in the middle of night, so some details might be blurry. Some altruistic race showed up 13,000 years ago and taught you all how to be better humans. Now you're paying it forward like any rich philanthropist would."

The Captain's brows shot up. "Ms. Nalawangsa also said you might have some very particular opinions of us, given the whole situation."

"It's been a long week for everyone, Captain." Lin offered. "Let's just cut each other some slack."

Nel shot her a grateful glance.

"Indeed." He turned back to his presentation. The next picture zoomed into the continent. It was less of a desert and more a wasteland. Something that would not look out of place on the set of a zombie apocalypse movie. "Well, the Teachers have ceased communication. We know where they last settled. Upon examination by satellite—" He tapped forward to the next image. It was a city. Even from however many kilometers above the surface the concentric circles of a blast radius were obvious "—we learned that they've disappeared. We're concerned whatever caused their disappearance may threaten us as well." The picture dissolved into the silver and yellow emblem of the Institute's Anthropology Department . "This is where you come in."

"I can't really see how that is."

"You're an archaeologist, aren't you? Sure, this culture isn't human, but excavation is excavation, am I right? You'll have state of the art equipment and experts in any field you need, including some you've never heard of."

Nel sat back, heart pounding. "You want me to do space archaeology."

"Yes. Will this be a problem?"

"No." Her voice sounded faint to her ears, as if it was projected from the surface of the planet she had just seen flashed over the screen before her. "I'm just wondering if I've been knocked unconscious and my favorite video games are surfacing as a hallucination." A small twinge of victory lit in her chest at the man's quickly hidden smile. Her thoughts sobered. "Why?"

"Excuse me?"

"Why did you pick me? I'm sure there were others who fit the bill. Those with fewer 'peculiar opinions' perhaps?"

"Don't be an ass, Nel." Lin hissed.

Dr. Sukarno snorted this time. "I think what she wants to know, Ms. Nalawangsa, is what made *you* think she was a good fit, out of the various candidates who came with fewer complications."

Nel glared at him. "Well, if I hadn't been framed for murder by you people it would have been easier, now wouldn't it." She looked over at Lin. "You've got this big Fixing-the-Humans gig. You were trained to do this since birth probably. I'm a hot-headed shovel-bum from Springfield, Maine."

Lin had the good grace to blush. "I wasn't chosen, it was part of my dissertation. I told you that. You make me sound pretentious."

"You're saving Earth just to get a PhD in Anthro from Space U. Doesn't get more pretentious than that."

"You were chosen because you already knew about this. Perhaps not all of it, but more than most. We run fewer risks, since you already know we exist. And you owe us, more than a bit, for clearing your name."

The snarky response Nel chambered about who framed her in the first place was drowned out by the PA system.

"Drs. Bently, Sukarno, Lieberman, and Ms. Nalawangsa and Mr. Addams, please report to the medical bay."

"Looks like we're out of time. Any of your other questions will be handled at Headquarters, I promise you." His gaze swiveled to Lin. "You can find your way to Medical?"

"Yes, sir." The feather press of Lin's hand on Nel's elbow raised her from the chair.

Nel's thoughts whirled, blocking out anything Lin might have said as she led them down two floors and across the complex. The base was built in circles. The wings radiated off the central hub that, Nel realized belatedly, housed the rocket. The medical bay was one of the larger wings, taking up two of the seven subterranean floors of the north wing. Instead of private exam rooms, however, they were ushered into curtained cubicles and ordered to strip. "Lin?"

"Yeah?" the other woman's voice arced over the teal curtain.

"Is this just a ploy to get me naked?" Nel hoped the other woman couldn't hear the tremor of nerves in her voice. The shaking rattled in her mind like an earthquake.

"Like I'd need a ploy."

Nel hung her jacket on the hook, touching the sleeve with reluctant fingers. Halfway through toeing off her boots, pain lanced up her foot. "Dammit. I'm still not used to this injured thing." The rest of her clothes she folded into her bag.

A purposeful knock rattled the metal frame of Nel's cubicle, and Dr. Gull's voice arced over the curtain. "Dr. Bently, may I come in?"

Nel glanced around for a johnny, but found none. She perched on the exam table and crossed her legs. As many woman had seen her naked, she still felt a flush creep up her face. "Yep."

"Hello again." Her smile was warm, if brief. "I've got to check a few things and see how your foot is doing, then you can be on your way." Her cold hands pressed several electrodes down the center line of Nel's body from brow to hips. She plugged the other end into what looked like a sleek tablet. The first scan looked like an X-ray, the second an ultrasound. The third was something that might have been infrared, but could have been anything. Gull's brows furrowed. "You're a bit malnourished."

"I was on the run for two months. It happens."

Her eyes met Nel's. "Oh. Of course." Her smile was shy. "You're impressive, Doctor. Got one hell of a pair on you."

"Uh, thanks." Nel looked away as the doctor knelt to examine her foot. She still couldn't bring herself to look at the limb.

"You're healing well. You need to eat more protein; it'll speed up the process. I'll put a note in your file about rations, all right?"

"Sounds good."

"Arm."

Nel offered her right arm, groaning when a loud click heralded a needle-stick. "I hate needles."

"Well, we can scan very small amounts of blood and tissue, so you're in luck. You only have to suffer the two. Until your next voyage, of course." She flicked through the tests as the tablet uttered a series of blips. "All clear." She held up something that looked like an epi-pen on steroids. "Inoculations then you're set."

"Can't I just risk the space-flu?"

Gull snorted. "If that's all it was I'd let you." She jabbed the pen against Nel's thigh.

The sting was replaced by burning as the vaccine filled her muscle. She yelped then glared at the woman. "All right, you're done."

"Sure am." She flashed a smile. "Keep those electrodes on, and thread this through the hole in the navel of your clothes." She unplugged the wires from her tablet and ended the end to Nel. "It'll hook you up to the life-scan of your suit. Have a safe flight, Dr. Bently."

Nel gripped the edge of the exam table for a minute after the doctor left. Her stomach churned in the aftermath of the injection. *I hate needles.*

"You all right?"

Nel glanced up to see Lin peering over the metal rail on top of the curtain. Her shoulders were bare, and Nel traced the shadow of her naked body on the curtain between them.

"You look better now that you're not a fugitive," Lin observed with a playful waggle of her dark brows.

"Thanks," Nel drawled. She jerked her thumb at the neatly folded pile of clothes on the edge of the bench. She recognized the material and style of Dr. Sukarno's track suit. "And here I thought it was just casual Friday."

Lin frowned and dropped back down into her cubicle. "It's a Wednesday, Nel."

"Never mind. How'd you guys know my size?"

"My hands remembered. And we've only got a few options. You're too buff for a small."

Nel's fingers faltered at the first sentence. She was used to going from lovers to strangers, but not to co-workers. "Right." She dragged on the silk leggings and tank. Over that came the tight-fitting black track suit. While the stripes on Sukarno's had been grey, Nel's were the same yellow as the Anthropology Department logo on the breast of the pullover. "I'm gonna sweat my ass off in these."

"You still have to put your suit on over them. Space is cold, you know."

Nel's motions stilled in their combing of her hair. *Space.* She stepped out from behind the screen. Lin was dressed similarly, though she still managed to look sleek, as opposed to a poorly-thought-out cosplayer. "You even make this get-up look good."

"Just wait until you see the suits. No one looks good in those."

"It's a fucking space suit, everyone looks awesome," Nel decided. She held up her bag and boots. "Where do I put these?"

"You'll have to check them when we're fitting for our suits."

"What is this, Delta?"

"Closer than you'd think." Lin jerked her head. "C'mon. We've only got a few more minutes." The floor at the bottom of Medical housed what seemed to be the costume rack of every space movie Hollywood ever made.

A foul-tempered man who reached Nel's shoulder took her name and shoved a garment bag at her. "Testing room's at the end of the hall."

Nel jogged after Lin and stepped into an airlock. A series of hoses hung from the ceiling, and several sinister buttons decorated a panel by the door.

"I don't think I'm going to like this."

"If you can't try your suit in a controlled environment how are you ever going to do this job?" Lin's brow arched. "Seriously, you'll hike alone and starving across New England while running from the police, but you're scared of actual nothing."

"Damn right." Nel watched the taller woman slip into her suit pieces and mimicked her. The pants came first, then the top. Metal and rubber gaskets rimmed the waist, wrists, and neck where the pieces joined. The whole was bulky and stiff, but Nel still felt naked in the face of a vacuum.

Lin glanced over. "Electrodes."

"Fuck." Nel wriggled out of the top and fumbled the wires out of her shirt and into the proper port. She pulled the shirt back on and locked it and her gloves in place. The helmet was last. The front half was clear, the glass thick and looked almost viscous, like a child's cup that held floating bits within the plastic. "What is this?"

"Liquid crystal. Tints and focuses so you can see in bright landscapes and zoom in. Before we all had corrective eye surgery, we could alter the prescription of the helmets too, for those who needed it. Glasses were too much of a liability."

"Shit." Nel glanced at Lin's gloves. "Your hands are different."

"This is my personal suit, outfitted to my preferences. It has bio-electrics built in."

"Like that glove thing you used to kill Bastian?"

Lin looked up, her eyes unreadable. She was quiet for a moment then shrugged. "It has a few other uses too, you know."

Nel looked away. "How do I work this?" She gestured to the helmet.

"Put it on. You can hear me through the coms." Lin did so first, showing her how to lock everything in place, then tapped a hard silver panel on her wrist. "This displays your suit's functions."

Nel barely heard half the words, her fingers ghosting over the controls. She hit something and a shrill beeping started. "Fuck!"

Lin grabbed her wrist and jabbed at something. "Don't mess with it. You would have depressurized your suit if you were in space."

"It's that easy?"

Lin smiled. "No, there are several fail-safes, but you have to treat everything as life and death when you're pressurized."

"I shouldn't be surprised by the level of tech anymore, but I am. I'm still picturing Neil and Buzz's get up."

Lin laughed. "This isn't NASA. They do wonderful work, but the world's disinterest in funding them is half the reason why IDH is around." She pulled down a set of hoses from the ceiling and motioned for Nel to do the same. "Everything is color coded and locks with a different shaped port. You can't screw it up." Her voice was both loud and intimate, humming through the helmet with a radio's static caress. "They clip to your left side, since you're a righty. Oxygen first. Filtration second.

Power third. Everything can run from batteries, which are charged by your movement, but if you have the ability to jack into a craft or structure's off board power, do so."

Nel slid the heavy green-labeled hose into the first port. The tank on her back stopped humming. Air hissed into her suit. Next came the blue hose, then black. The lights on her com and helmet brightened, and the panel on her arm blinked a notification that all systems were using external resources.

"Nice job." Lin's smile looked plastic through the layers of glass. "You're ready."

"Seriously?"

"Ready as you can be. Let's get going." Her deft hands had detached her hoses and unclipped her helmet by the time Nel unfastened her oxygen. Nel fell into lurching ski-boot step behind her, glancing back once to be sure her pack and bag of affects were loaded onto the proper luggage cart.

They emerged into the hub of the building and ascended to the eighth floor. A series of telescoping walkways bridged the gap to the open door of the craft itself. The scurry of mechanics and robotic levers grew more frantic. Lin leaned on the rail overlooking the sunken floor. Her black braid looped on itself and disappeared under the snug silk cap that went under their helmets. "It's because you ran."

"What?"

Lin met Nel's eyes. "The reason I told them to bring you. You were faced with a terrible choice. We asked you to run, and you did. I knew you would. So here I am asking you to run again. I knew you'd say yes. I still have no idea why, but that doesn't matter."

"The story."

It was Lin's turn to tilt her head. "To tell to people?"

"No. The other one. I'm an explorer. Everyone is, on some level. That's why I dig. I'm looking for the why, the how, the where. And this is just about the biggest exploration I could dream up." Nel drew a deep breath and closed her eyes. The launch lights blazed through her eyelids, searing her retinas with the silhouette of blood vessels. "When do we board."

"Three minutes. They're finishing the first round of pre-flight tests."

Nel glanced up at the massive doors as they ground open. "How do you explain this? Do you chalk it up to NASA?"

"No one watches launches anymore, least wise, no one who anyone would listen to if they started claiming we weren't what we said. But yeah, it's either NASA or SpaceX."

"And you've done this before?" As excited as she was, nerves were a hot knot in Nel's gut.

"Launched from Earth once. Launched from Headquarters a few times, though it's different when you don't have to break atmo. Less climactic. I was mostly on Dar's ship, or my parents'."

"Will I meet them?"

"I assume so, at some point. They might be at the briefing, though depends on their rotation." She shrugged. "We don't get to talk much when I'm planet-side."

Nel shook her head. "Until the last few months I hadn't gone more than a week without talking to my mom." She blanched. *Fuck, I have to call her.* "I've gotta take care of something real quick."

"Nel, this isn't a commercial flight. We can't wait for you." The blare of a klaxon cut off whatever else Lin was about to say. When it was through, she jerked her head at the craft. "We're loading up."

"It's important. It'll take just a minute, I promise."

"Make it quick."

Nel flashed a grin of thanks at Lin's grudging nod and ducked into a quieter hallway. She flicked her phone open and dialed two. Her call went straight to her mom's voicemail.

"I don't have a ton of time, but I wanted to call. You asked me not to disappear again, but it looks like I might. Not for good, and not for a terrible reason this time. It's for the job. I can't tell you more. I want to, but I can't." Above, the countdown blared. Lin popped her head around the corner.

"C'mon, time's up." She jerked her head at the space shuttle.

Nel nodded and cupped the phone to block out the worst of the background noise. "I've got to go. I'm OK. I love you. I'll miss you." She tapped the red phone icon and slid the phone into the pocket in the abdomen of the suit. She always hated goodbyes, but after Mikey, she understood their importance far more than before. The space missions she read about in the news lasted months. Some lasted years.

"Nel!" Lin stood at the entrance to the causeway.

"Coming." The walk across the open metal slats seemed to take both forever and just the single blink of Nel's suddenly watering eyes. The doorway was circular, some Kubrick version of Bilbo's front door. *Mind your feet, Bently.* She followed Lin up the ladder in what clearly would be the "floor" when they were in zero gravity. An aisle led through the double banks of seats. Most were occupied.

"I didn't realize it'd be so crowded."

Lin grinned. "We're in the front, but I think we'll have a window." She pointed. "Yep. Here we are. You first."

Nel sidled in using the bars provided and tucked herself into the chair's embrace. "Do I get a plastic cup of champagne and some peanuts, too?" The man in the row under them shot her an irritated glare, which she ignored. Instead, she counted the passengers. "This bigger than most missions?"

"Smaller. The usual trips carry close to a hundred." Lin smiled. "Wait until you see Headquarters. And the big ships. They're like continents." She settled herself into the seat with ease, and Nel rolled her eyes.

"Helmet?" she asked.

"On. Everything on." Lin pointed to the hoses coiled on hooks along the wall. "Hook up and buckle yourself in. That chest piece attaches to the center of the buckle. Yeah, that's it."

Nel fastened the buckles and tightened the five-point harness around herself before leaning her head back. The helmet muffled most of the cabin noises, but Lin's voice chimed in Nel's ear through the tiny headphone as she explained the additional communications features when a suit was hooked into a ship's system. Nel only half-listened, the other part of her mind watching the others filtering in around them. Beeping cut through Lin's explanation of the volume.

"Hello everyone and welcome to the *Iman*. Please take this time to check that you are properly hooked in. Our Launch Engineer can help you with any questions. We'll be igniting in T-2 minutes. Please remain in your seat at all times during flight. Our lift-off speeds exceed 29,000 kilometers per hour and there is a chance you may fall unconscious. When gravitational levels and acceleration return to normal, you will regain consciousness. Our journey will take just under two days and we will dock at the International Space Station at approximately 26:30 Base Time. You will be briefed upon your arrival. Please switch all communications devices to travel settings. Enjoy your ride."

Nel stared at Lin and pressed the mic button. "This can't be real. That sounded like a joke from Southwest."

"Travel is travel." She reached over and typed a few numbers into Nel's wrist display then hit a green button. "There, now you're just talking to me. Were you listening at all, earlier?"

Nel snorted. "Forgive me if I'm a bit distracted by the fact that I'm in a fucking space shuttle." A blue digital clock on the wall before her suddenly blinked on: 0:20. The craft jolted. Outside the window the floor was cleared, save for several of the massive machines. She caught sight of faces peering through the glass of the offices at the shuttle.

0:14.

With a roar, the ship began to tremble, like a mechanical stretch at dawn. Nel's pocket buzzed. Her gloved fingers fumbled the phone out and flipped it open. It was her mother.

I LOVE YOU TOO, IS EVERYTHIHNG OK? WHERE ARE THEY SENDING YOU?

Nel lifted the phone and snapped a picture of Lin, decked out in her space suit. She ignored the woman's glare and sent the image with a caption:

YOU'LL NEVER BELIEVE ME.

She powered the phone down and tightened her belts for the third time. The countdown flashed green.

0:03.

The engines ignited with a roar.

END

Here's a look at the third of the Nel Bently Books:

STRANGERS

Nel stared at the tiny cubicle. Spartan would be a generous term. *And would imply more character than the black and grey walls offered.* Lin had disappeared, presumably to settle into her own coffin-like bedroom. Nel glanced at the small aluminum case ion the desk. All of her possessions, the ones she would use for the next who-knew-how-long. The closet above the desk held three outfits, al along the track-suit line of fashion. She wasn't able to bring enough to personalize the space. If the space even allowed for it. *TIME alone in this room, with only Lin to talk to.* She heaved a sigh and slumped onto the bed. She opened the case and carefully dug out the tissue-wrapped boxes that help Mikey and her father's ashes. *Only the necessities.*

Lin stepped into the room. Her face was smooth, devoid of expression. Her eyes were the black of space. They, too, were lit with strange stars. "We need to talk."

"I hate that phrase."

"Like I'm going to break up with you when we're stuck on a space ship together." Lin's tone was strained, despite her attempt at humor.

Nel winced at the term. She had not been under the impression that there was something to break up. "So what is it?"

"You've signed a contract. A binding one."

"Why are you reminding me?"

"So you remember you can't break it."

Nel's limbs ignited with adrenaline. "You gonna give me a reason to want to?"

Lin looked away. "Space travel is complicated. We have incredible technology. We can go beyond the limits of physics. But not time. Even with our faster-than-light tech it can take a long time to get where we want to go. It took three years for us to get to earth the first time."

Nel looked out the window at the scattered balls of burning hydrogen, made pinpricks by thousands of light years. She couldn't have drawn the sky over her parents' house in Springfield by heart, or the starscape above the red hills of Chile from memory. But he animal parts of her, the subconscious observations that were called sixth sense, knew. *The stars are all wrong.* "Lin, where are we?"

"We're approaching *Promise*, which is in deep orbit around the planet we're studying."

"And *Promise* is the space station?"

Lin nodded. *"Promise for Tomorrow."* Her dark eyes had not met Nel's since the taller woman first uttered "time."

"And how far is that from Earth?"

"117.3 trillion kilometers."

Nel didn't know space like she knew soil and stone. She spent her life looking down, not up, digging not dreaming. She did not know what 117.3 trillion kilometers meant, only that her blood was a storm in her ears and the sky was not hers. "And for how long was I out?"

"Two years."

The floor pitched, tilting with a viciousness that had nothing to do with artificial gravity. "You're telling me I was locked in that tube for years, asleep like all of some tinned fish in the back of a cabinet?"

Look for *Strangers* from Amphibian Press in 2018!

Here's a look at the first in a series of short stories that take place in the Nel Bently Universe:

STARFALL

Clacking heels were once empowering. They announced Andy's presence like a battle-cry. Now she wanted to plug her ears with the clank of every other footstep. She balanced the box of her things on the counter's edge as she fumbled for her new yellow ID. "Sorry, Madge, it's been a shite day."

The older woman glanced up, eye's sympathetic. "I'll need your passcard too, Andy. I never expected them to can you. Is it over that article the other week?"

Andy winced. There were no lies thick enough to hide the truth. Even if Madge somehow missed the glaring yellow of the ID, she'd see the biomech leg as Andy walked away. "I had an accident." She refused to look up, to face the awkward judgment and sympathy brought by the 'MECH' stamped across the card.

"Well if you need anything, sweetie—"

"I'll keep it in mind, thanks." Andy shoved herself away from the counter and towards the door. *Tap-clank. Tap-clank.* She forced her chin up as she crossed the lobby of Planet-8 News. Her curiosity had always been a boon as a journalist. She just never thought it would get her fired. One pointed question about bio-mechs, one transport bomb, one amputation was all it took. She was suddenly part of the exact marginalized community she had been investigating.

Her com buzzed on her wrist. Once, twice, a dozen insistent beeps by the time she reached the transport station. She found a seat in the corner and perched the box on her lap before tapping her com's screen.

(1) CONFIRMATION OF EMPLOYMENT TERMINATION

(2) FAILURE OF LEASE AGREEMENT

(3) TERMINATION OF LEASE DUE TO UNEMPLOYMENT

(4) NOTIFICATION OF WHERE TO RETRIEVE BELONGINGS

Andy unclipped the com and threw it across the transport with a frustrated snarl. She looked away from the alarmed stares. This was ridiculous. One mechanical leg and her boss thought she was inhuman. That she couldn't perform her job. The economy wasn't bad, but clearly the likelihood of a bio-mech finding a job was dismal enough for her to lose her apartment.

"APPROACHING AEROSPACE HUB. ARRIVAL 13:45."

The blackness of the transport tunnel fell away as the capsule glided through the massive expanse of the largest port on Earth. Gleaming titanium was acceptable here, revered even. As long as it wasn't attached to blood and breathing flesh. The capsule slowed to a hissing stop and the doors slid open.

"ARRIVED AT AEROSPACE HUB BAKJEERI. NEXT STOP, KAUSHAMBI. DEPARTURE IN ONE MINUTE."

No job. No home. 2670 United in her credit account. Andy shoved the box off her lap and shouldered through the doors of the capsule before she could change her mind.

Starfall was previously published alone in *Vitality Magazine* in January of 2016. Look for the completed anthology from Amphibian Press soon!

ACKNOWLEDGEMENTS

This book would not have made it without the help of some amazing people, far more than I could list here.

But this is a start.

Thank you to Marissa for always pushing me and talking me out of the tree, and for the use of her awesome character, Tabby.

Thank you to my awesome editor, Angie, for your feedback and support.

Thank you to my archaeologist friends and family-by-choice for your incredible love of life and energy, and for continuing to inspire me every day.

ABOUT THE AUTHOR

V. S. Holmes lives in a Tiny House and owns too many books for such a small abode. Her favorite genres include fantasy, science (of both the non-fiction and fiction varieties), and anything with diverse protagonists.

Holmes graduated from Keene State College with a Bachelors of Science in Biology. She has a particular interest in prehistoric peoples and stone tools. When not writing, she works as a contract archaeologist doing Cultural Resource Management throughout the northeastern U.S.

Smoke and Rain, the first in her fantasy quartet, was chosen for New Apple Literary's 2015 Excellence in Independent Publishing Award. *Starfall*, a science-fiction short can be found in the January 2016 issue of *Vitality*, an LGBT magazine.

76483312R00140

Made in the USA
Columbia, SC
10 September 2017